A division of Hodder Headline Limited

For Tamar Brazis
(and Guy's fans Natty, Alex, Henry and Max)

First published in the USA in 2001
as 'My Guy' by HarperCollins Children's Books

First published in Great Britain in 2004
by Hodder Children's Books

10 9 8 7 6 5 4 3 2 1

ISBN 0 340 86614 4

Typeset by Avon DataSet Ltd, Bidford-on-Avon, Warwickshire

Printed and bound in Great Britain by
Bookmarque Ltd., Croydon, Surrey

Hodder Children's Books
a division of Hodder Headline Limited
338 Euston Road
London NW1 3BH

CHAPTER ONE

'I knew this was going to happen. I just knew it,' I said when Buzz and I met on the corner to walk to school together.

'What?' he said, yanking up his sleeve to look at his watch. 'Am I late?'

'I'm not talking about punctuality, you cornflake. I'm talking about life and death.'

'Well, I'm glad *you* know what you're talking about, Guy, because I sure don't.'

I didn't see any point in beating around the bush. Buzz is my best friend, and I tell him everything. Even the awful stuff. Like this horrible piece of news.

'My mother is getting married,' I said.

Buzz stopped in his tracks and turned to look

at me. '*What?* Oh, man. Please tell me she isn't gonna marry that dork Brad.'

'No,' I said. 'Worse than Brad.'

'Come on. Who could be worse than Brad?' asked Buzz. 'The man winks and has a wallet made out of fur.'

'Trust me, *Jerry* is worse than Brad,' I said.

'Who's Jerry?'

'Jerry Zuckerman.' I kicked a stone and sent it skipping out into the street.

'Who's Jerry Zuckerman?'

'*Zuckerman*, you trout. Does it ring a bell?' I said.

'Not really,' said Buzz. 'The only Zuckerman I know is Lana.'

'Exactly.'

'Exactly what?' he asked.

'Jerry Zuckerman is Lana Zuckerman's father.'

Buzz screwed up his face in disbelief.

'Your mother is marrying *our* Lana Zuckerman's father?'

I nodded.

'Sheesh,' Buzz said with appropriate feeling.

I've known Lana Zuckerman since kindergarten, when she used to torture me by calling me 'Girlie Guy' because of the pink mittens my mother made me for Christmas that year.

'Pink is a girl's colour,' I said with utter dismay as I stared at the mittens on Christmas morning.

'Oh, pooh,' my mother said. 'How can someone own a colour? Look at your skin, Guysie. It's pink. And you're a boy, aren't you? That pink and blue business is just nonsense. I don't believe in it.'

Well, I believed in it, and apparently so did Lana Zuckerman and the rest of the kids in her crowd. The day I wore those mittens to school, they chased me around the playground yelling, 'Girlie Guy! Girlie Guy! Let's have a tea party!' until finally the teacher came out and called them off. I accidentally 'lost' the mittens down the sewer grate on the way home from school that day. But losing the unpleasant memory has proved to be a lot harder.

From kindergarten on, somehow Lana and I

ended up in the same class every year until we went to middle school. She was always the tallest kid in the class, boy or girl. She towered over everyone, and anyone who tangled with her once knew enough to avoid doing it again. She's as mean as a snake and about equally appealing.

Buzz moved to town when we were all in second grade, but Lana didn't take much notice of him. By then she'd decided that all boys were beneath her, which, because of her height, was absolutely true. To her we were all just a bunch of puny, worthless little balls of crud, to use her exact words. Fine with me. I was more than happy to be ignored by her. I knew she was dangerous.

Then last year a pretty bizarre thing happened. It's kind of a long story, but I guess in a way I started it by having a crush on this girl Autumn Hockney. At first, Buzz thought I was crazy to like a girl. I wasn't all that sure it was such a good idea myself, but Buzz was so upset by it that he threatened to tie me to a kitchen chair and keep me there until he had managed to talk some sense into me. Then, much to my surprise, he changed his mind about girls and got a crush on one himself. That girl turned out to be none other than Lana Zuckerman. It seemed like a crazy match to me. I couldn't figure out why Buzz, who is one of my favourite people on earth, would be interested in Lana. But he likes her. And she likes him right back.

'So Mr Zuckerman and your mom are getting married? I can't believe it. Sheesh, Guy, this is big. Is he gonna dump Mrs Zuckerman the First to make room for your mom?' Buzz asked as we continued on towards school.

'The Zuckermans are divorced, you flounder. Remember? Lana lives with her dad except in the summer, when she goes out to California to live with her mom.'

'Oh yeah, I forgot,' he said. 'She doesn't talk about it much.'

I could relate. My parents have been divorced for about a year and I hardly ever talk about it. What is there to say, really? It just is. The way it worked out, I basically live with my mother, because my dad travels a lot for his job. I call her house 'home'. But I spend a lot of time at my dad's house too. When he's around, I can see him whenever I want, spend the night or weekends with him and usually school vacations, too. At first it was hard having my parents living in two different houses, even though they're only a few blocks away from each other, but eventually I got used to it and now I don't mind too much.

'Okay, so let me ask you a question,' Buzz said as we rounded the corner and headed down the last block toward school. 'Is this necessarily bad news? I mean, couldn't there be something good about it?'

'For instance?' I said.

'Well, maybe Lana's dad is a nice guy. I know you don't like Lana, but it's possible her dad is okay, right? And you know how people are always saying it's good to have a man around the house. They must be saying it for a reason.'

'Like what?' I asked.

'I don't know, maybe because a man could, like, lift stuff for you and your mom.'

'Lift stuff? What kind of stuff are you talking about?' I said.

'I don't know, heavy stuff. Like for instance, the people next door to me – you know, the ones in the big house – well, they moved out last week, and I saw Mr Peterson out there pushing his piano all by himself down the driveway to the truck. The guy's got arms like Popeye. Unfortunately, he's got the personality of a grapefruit, so hopefully whoever moves in next will be a little friendlier, but anyway, where was I? Oh yeah, the point is, maybe Jerry is strong and could, you know, like, move a piano for you guys or something.'

'In case you haven't noticed, Nimrod, we don't have a piano,' I said.

'In case *you* haven't noticed, Nimrod, this is *me* you're talking to here, not some horsefly who deserves to have his intelligence insulted just because you happen to be in a one hundred per cent totally rotten mood,' Buzz said.

'I'm sorry, Buzzard. You're right.'

'Aw, it's okay,' he said. 'What's a Nimrod, anyway?'

'I'm not sure. I just like the way it sounds. So I admit I'm grumpy, but cut me a little slack, okay? I'm pretty freaked out over this news.'

'Yeah, I know. That's why I was trying to come up with something positive to say about Jerry Zuckerman.'

'Well, other than the possibility that he might be able to lift a piano, can you think of any other reason why I should be happy about my mother marrying him?'

'Only what I said before. Maybe he's a nice guy. Someone who'd be okay to have around,' Buzz said.

'Let's just talk about my mother's dating record for a second. Every single guy she's gone out with since my parents split up has been – what?'

'Strange,' Buzz answered.

'So what does that tell you about Jerry Zuckerman?'

'Well, nothing for *sure*,' Buzz hedged.

I looked at him.

'Okay, there's a pretty good chance that he's weird,' he said.

'On top of that, his daughter is, well, *Lana*. You do see the significance of that, don't you?'

'I don't know why you can't see the good stuff about Lana. Once you get past the fact that she's sort of bossy and grouchy, and she sometimes punches people, she's really pretty terrific. She's got a good sense of humour, and she can do seventy-five push-ups without even breaking a sweat. How many girls do you know who can do that?'

'How many *girls*? I can't do that, and face it, neither can you.'

'True, but that's not even the point. The point is, so what if you two don't get along that well? You're not the ones getting married,' Buzz said.

'Think about it, Buzzard. If our parents get married, they'll want to live together, right? And if they live together, that means Lana and I are going to have to live together too, right? That's a whole lot closer to being married to her than I ever want to be,' I said.

'Okay, I see what you mean. I hadn't thought about it like that.'

'Well, I have, and it makes me sick. You remember how hard it was at first when my parents split up? Now that I'm used to it and everything is sort of normal again, why does my mom have to go screwing things up?'

We walked in silence for a while. Then Buzz asked, 'Have they set a wedding date?'

'Valentine's Day,' I said with disgust.

'Repulse-o-rama,' said Buzz. 'And she just popped it on you this morning with no warning?'

'Well, I guess I should have known something bad was coming,' I said.

'Ohhh,' Buzz groaned. 'Let me guess, did she make you . . .?' He raised his eyebrows and looked at me.

I nodded.

Some people believe that black cats or broken mirrors can bring you bad luck. Lately, for me, it's homemade waffles.

CHAPTER TWO

I used to love my mother's homemade waffles with strawberries and whipped cream more than almost anything else in the world. She'd make them for me every year on my birthday and for other special occasions during the year too. But the last time she made them was when she told me that she and my dad were splitting up. That was one of the worst days of my life, and I guess she probably did it because she thought the waffles would soften the blow. Anyway, when I came downstairs the morning she broke the news about marrying Jerry Zuckerman, the plate of steaming waffles at my place should have tipped me off right away that something terrible was about to happen.

'Guysie, I've got something very exciting to tell you,' she said as I slipped into my seat and put my napkin in my lap.

'Yeah? What?' I took the cap off the can of whipped cream and squirted some directly into my mouth.

'Shame on you!' She laughed and snatched it away. She made a little mountain of cream on top of the waffles, kissed the top of my head, then went to the kitchen to get the bowl of cut-up strawberries to sprinkle on top.

'Dig in,' she said with a big smile.

She sat down and watched me take a huge bite of waffles.

'So, do you want to hear my news?' she asked.

I shrugged and kept chewing. I was busy with my fork, setting up the next perfect bite with just the right balance of waffle, cream, and berry.

'I'm getting married,' she said.

I choked and sprayed the entire mouthful of chewed-up waffle all over the table.

'What?' I yelled as soon as I'd caught my breath.

My mother got a sponge from the sink and calmly wiped the table.

'On February fourteenth, this Valentine's Day, Jerry and I are tying the knot.'

'Who the heck is Jerry?' I said.

'Well, this is the part that may take some getting used to, Guysie. You see, Jerry is Lana's father.'

I looked at her.

'Not Lana *Zuckerman*,' I whispered in the kind of voice you might use if you were speaking of a convicted axe murderer who'd just escaped from prison and had been spotted lurking in your backyard.

She nodded.

'I know it's a little shocking, honeybunch.'

'A little?' I said. 'How did this happen?'

'Well, let's see. Jerry and I met at a PTA meeting last spring, and we liked each other right off the bat. He is such a hoot. You know how I love a man with a sense of humour, and they are *so* hard to find. Anyway, we dated up a storm during the summer while you were at camp and Lana was out in California with her mom, and by the time September rolled around, we just kind of knew we were meant to be,' she said.

I listened to her talking and watched her wide red lips forming the words as she went along, but I couldn't believe what I was hearing. She was talking about this man she'd basically been dating behind my back for months and was now planning to marry even though his daughter and I hated each other's guts, in the same way she might rattle on about a new pair of shoes she'd picked up on sale at The Shoe Box in the mall. Didn't she realise that this was earth-shattering news to me? Didn't she realise that this was about the worst thing that could possibly happen to my life?

'I would have told you earlier, Guysie, but we were both worried that it might make things uncomfortable for you and Lana at school.'

My mother completely blows my mind on a regular basis, and this was one of those times. How could she stand there and say she was worried about making me *uncomfortable*? Generally speaking, when someone ruins your life, it's not a comfortable experience.

'Does Dad know?' I asked. My father had been out of the country on business for the past two weeks, but I wondered if she'd called him to tell him the news.

'Yes. I reached him in Barcelona last night. He was just great about it. He's really happy for me.'

'What about Lana? Does she know yet?' I asked.

'Jerry's telling her this morning.'

Needless to say, I'd lost my taste for waffles. For ever. I pushed my chair back and went to get my backpack.

'Isn't this exciting, Guysie? I mean, I know it's kind of sudden, but Jerry's a wonderful guy. I just know you two are going to get along like gangbusters. And even though you and Lana aren't the best of friends – I remember that silly business about pink mittens way back when – I'm sure she's mellowed with age.'

Oh yeah. Lana is about as mellow as a flaming cannonball.

'It might be nice to have a sister around the house,' she said. 'Ever thought about that?'

'It might be nice to have a rabid raccoon around the house too. Ever thought about *that*?' I said.

'And I've always wondered what it would be like to have a daughter,' my mother sighed dreamily, without even stopping to let the rabid raccoon comment sink in.

It made my skin crawl hearing my mother get all moony about having a daughter. What in the world did she think she could do with Lana that she couldn't do with me?

'Lana's already got a mother,' I said. 'She lives in California, you know.'

'Uh-huh, I know,' my mother said, and barrelled right on. 'I don't know if you know this about me, Guy, but even though things didn't work out between your father and me, the truth is, I'm one of those people who believe in marriage. I'm very gung-ho about giving it another try. We're going to be one big happy family!'

'Like *that's* gonna happen,' I said. 'Lana and me being part of one big happy family is about as likely as sticking a fork into our backyard and striking oil.'

'Oh, Guysie,' she said, 'I know you feel that way now, but give it a little time. I'm sure you'll come around to seeing things our way.'

'Whose way is "our way"?' I asked.

'Jerry's and mine,' she said. 'We have the utmost faith in you and Lana, and we're both so darned tickled about this that we could just bust.'

Every time she said *we* or *us* or *our*, it felt like someone was sticking a pin in me.

'So that's my big news, Guysie – what do you think?'

'I think I don't ever want to see another one of your homemade waffles again as long as I live,' I said.

Then I zipped up my jacket, slung my backpack over my shoulder, and headed out the door to go meet Buzz. My mother was standing in the kitchen with a confused look on her face and a spatula in her hand. As I left, she mournfully called after me, 'But I thought you loved my waffles.'

CHAPTER THREE

I'll say one thing for Lana Zuckerman – she's not afraid to say what's on her mind.

'I swear, Guy Strang, if you say one word to me about this business with my father and your mother, I'm going to give you such a pinch, you'll howl like a little monkey boy.'

She was out in front of the school when Buzz and I got there, and I could tell even from a distance that she was in a foul mood. She kept pounding her right fist into her left palm like she was getting ready to punch someone.

'Come on, Lana, give Guy a break. He's just as freaked out about it as you are,' said Buzz.

'I doubt it,' she said, sneering at me.

'What's going on?' asked Bob-o as he joined us in the yard.

'Lana's dad and Guy's mom are getting married,' said Buzz.

'Yeah, right,' he snorted, and pushed his glasses up on his nose.

Bob-o has always been kind of the class nerd, and because of that he's spent most of his time out of the loop, socially speaking. Buzz and I discovered a few years back that, underneath his oddness (and believe me, there is a *lot* of oddness), he's actually a pretty nice guy. But because of his long-standing nerd status, he still has a tendency to think that people are fooling with him even when they're not.

'No, really, I'm not kidding, Bob-o,' said Buzz. 'They're tying the knot on Valentine's Day.'

'Valentine's Day. That is *so* gross,' Lana said. Then she turned to me. 'You know whose brilliant idea *that* was, don't you?'

She grabbed my jacket and pulled me up until we were at eye level, which meant that the tips of my sneakers were just barely touching the ground.

'You *know*, don't you?' she asked again.

I shook my head, even though I had a feeling I knew exactly whose idea it had been.

'Your *mother's*,' she said through gritted teeth.

'I can't help it if she's corny,' I said.

She glared at me, and for a second I wondered if she was going to punch me. Then she let go of me and I dropped back down to the ground, taking a couple of steps backwards to keep my balance.

'Here comes Autumn,' Buzz said, poking me in the ribs and pointing across the yard.

The year before, just the mention of her name would have sent me around the twist, I was so crazy about her, but Autumn and I came uncrushed over the summer. It was kind of a mutual thing, I guess. She wrote to me once at camp, and somehow I didn't get around to writing her back. I made her a wallet in arts and crafts, but I ended up giving it to my dad because by the time I came home, Autumn had developed a new crush on someone else – namely, Maxwell LaMott. At first when I found out about it, it bugged me a little. But I'm over that now. Mostly, anyway.

'What's the matter?' Autumn asked when she got close enough to see Lana's face.

Lana took Autumn aside and quickly filled her in on the news. I couldn't hear what she was saying, but as she spoke, she kept jabbing her thumb in my direction and giving me dirty looks. Autumn shook her head and looked over at me a couple of times too.

'It's not like it's my fault!' I called out to them. 'This marriage isn't my idea, you know.'

'Calm down, Guy Wire,' Buzz said, patting my back.

But I didn't feel calm at all. My insides felt like they'd been tied in a fat knot, and those waffles I'd had for breakfast were sitting in a big chewed-up wad right on top.

'So, do you think you and Lana will be invited to the wedding?' Bob-o asked me.

'If I am, I'm not going,' I said.

'What's gonna happen after the wedding?' asked Bob-o.

'What do you mean, after? Like on the honeymoon?' asked Buzz.

I felt a sick twinge in the pit of my stomach.

'No, I mean after all of that mushy stuff. You know, when the party's over and real life sets in. Looks like you guys are going to be related,' Bob-o said.

'Who's going to be related?' Lana asked as she shoved me aside and joined the group again.

'You and Guy,' said Bob-o. 'Are you going to hyphenate your last names? Which do you think sounds better: Zuckerman-Strang or Strang-Zuckerman?'

'Which do you think sounds better: a punch in the stomach or a—' All of a sudden Lana stopped talking and started making a weird wheezing sound. Like she couldn't catch her breath.

'What's the matter with her?' asked Bob-o.

'Look at her, she's turning all red,' said Buzz with alarm.

'She's going to puke!' I cried, quickly taking a big step backward.

'No . . . you . . . idiots. It's . . . my . . . asthma!' Lana managed to get out between wheezes. 'Quick . . . get me . . . a bag . . .'

Autumn starting emptying her pockets, pulling out Chap Stick and gum and all sorts of other stuff, but no bag. Then Buzz threw his backpack on the ground, tore it open, and pulled out his lunch. He dumped it out on the ground and quickly handed Lana the brown paper bag. She fastened it over her mouth and nose and started breathing into it.

'Sheesh, Lana,' Buzz said. 'Sheesh.' I could tell he was scared. We all were. We hovered over Lana until, as we watched with relief, her face slowly returned to its normal colour. After a couple of minutes she was breathing normally again.

'Your bag smells like meat loaf,' Lana said, handing the bag back to Buzz.

'What do you expect? It was an emergency. Look at the sacrifice I made,' he said, indicating the lunch that lay on the ground all trampled and smushed. 'I love my mother's meat-loaf sandwiches.'

'I'll treat you to lunch in the cafeteria, Buzzer,' Lana said.

'Some treat,' he snorted.

Lana laughed, but then she turned to me, and her face was grimmer than ever.

'I want you to know I have no intention whatsoever of being your sister,' she said.

'Technically, you'd be Guy's stepsister,' offered Bob-o.

'Technically, I'll knock your teeth down your throat if you say something stupid like that again,' she said to him. 'Now, back to you, Guy Strang. You are not going to be my brother, do you hear me?'

I didn't know what to say. I mean, the thought of being related to Lana Zuckerman was just as upsetting to me as it was to her. In fact, at that moment I couldn't imagine anything much worse.

'What does she expect me to do? Break them up and ruin the wedding plans?' I said, turning to Buzz in anguish. 'How am I supposed to do that?'

'Do you hear me, Girlie Guy?' she said. 'Do you?'

I heard her. But I wasn't really listening. Her obnoxious voice was being drowned out by the sound of my only hope – the gears slowly beginning to turn in Buzz's head as a very familiar look spread across his face.

CHAPTER FOUR

'All right, let's have it,' I said as we walked home after school that day. 'I've been waiting all day for this.'

'What? I already gave you back that buck I borrowed last week. Remember?'

'Not that, you Cocoa Puff. I'm talking about the plan. I know you're cooking something up. So tell me already.'

'Oh, that. Well, it's not completely thought out yet.'

'What have you got so far?' I asked.

I knew Buzz was trying to think up a plan the minute I saw that look on his face in the school yard. Plans are Buzz's speciality. Actually, they're *our* speciality, but Buzz is always the one who starts the ball rolling.

'Okay, we have to convince them that getting married is a bad idea because the four of you would never be able to get along well enough to live together. Right?' he said.

'Yeah,' I said, motioning with my hands for him to go on.

'That's all I've got so far.'

'That is the opposite of impressive, Buzzard. I'm counting on you here. Lana and I already don't get along, and it hasn't stopped our parents from getting engaged. Come on – don't you have anything more than that?'

'Calm down, calm down. This is complicated, but I'll come up with something. I don't know what yet, but something. Have I ever let you down?'

'Never,' I said. 'And this would not be the time to break that streak.'

There was snow on the ground, and the air was so cold, it hurt your face to be outside for more than two seconds.

'How much homework do you have?' he asked.

'Not much. I've got maths, a worksheet for science, plus current events,' I answered.

'Same for me. Hey, do you think your mother's engagement could count as a current event?' Buzz asked as we stamped our snowy boots on the back-porch steps of my house.

We always go to my house after school because the food's better. Buzz's mom is nice, but she thinks rice cakes are a good snack and raisins are a treat. We went inside, pulled off our boots and jackets, dropped our backpacks on the floor, and headed for the cookie jar. Buzz got there first. He closed his eyes as he lifted off the top and reached in.

'Oh please, oh please, oh please let there be snicker doodles,' he said softly.

Buzz lives for my mother's cookies.

'Yoo-hoo, boys!' my mother called from the other room. 'If you're looking for something yummy, check the bottom shelf in the fridge. I made a little experiment.'

Buzz opened his eyes, pulled his empty hand out of the jar, and looked at me. My mother's experiments are a mixed bag. Every now and then she makes something great, like the giant peanut butter cookies she baked on the barbecue grill. They looked a little weird, but boy, were they good. Then there are the less successful attempts, like the vegetable brownies and the yogurt candy.

'What did you make this time?' I called out to her.

'Chocolate dumplings,' she called back.

At least the chocolate part sounded promising. Buzz opened the fridge and squatted down to look at the bottom shelf.

'How do they look?' I asked.

He pulled out a plate with four huge white balls on it. He brought it over to the kitchen counter and set it down. We stared at it.

'They sure are big,' he said.

'And white,' I said.

'And lumpy. Maybe we should cut one open. She said there was chocolate in them, right?' Buzz opened the drawer and pulled out a long knife.

He sliced one of the balls in half, and a grainy orange liquid spilled out of it onto the plate.

'Sheesh, what's that disgusting junk?' Buzz asked.

'For your information, that disgusting junk is imported marmalade filling,' my mother said from the doorway.

'I thought you said they were *chocolate* dumplings,' I said.

'They are. That's white chocolate on the outside.'

Buzz took a small piece of the white coating and sniffed it, but he didn't put it in his mouth. He just set it gently back on the plate.

'Go ahead, Buzzy,' she said. 'Taste it.'

'No offence, but I'm not what you'd call a big marmalade fan,' he said.

'Who is?' I said. 'How come you didn't fill them with something good, Mom?'

'Marmalade is good,' she said. 'It's as popular in London as grape jelly is over here.'

I wasn't about to waste my time arguing with her. Not with a woman who thinks sardines and peanut butter are a 'heavenly combination' and black liquorice is 'the perfect way to perk up any dish' – including salad and hot cereal.

Buzz and I just stood there looking sadly at the oozing white ball on the plate.

'Oh, suit yourselves,' she said, reaching into a cupboard. 'Here. Have a bag of pretzels, straight from the factory, untouched by human hands, just the way you like them.'

'Thanks,' I said, taking the bag from her. 'Grab two cans of soda, will you, Buzzard? Let's go.'

'Hold on a sec. Where's the fire?' she asked, reaching out and taking hold of my shoulders. I shrugged out of her hands.

'We've got homework, Mom.'

'Can't we chat for a minute first? I want to know how it went with Lana today. Did she say anything?'

'Mom,' I moaned.

My mother turned to Buzz.

'I assume Guy told you my garbanzo news,' she said.

'Garbanzo?' said Buzz. 'Isn't that a kind of bean?'

'*Garbanzo* means "wonderful" in Mom's private language,' I explained. 'The one the aliens taught her when they abducted her and replaced her brain with a half-melted pudding pop.'

'Very funny. Now really, what do you think about it, Buzzy?'

'About you marrying Lana's dad? To tell you the truth, I've never met Mr Zuckerman, but I know Lana pretty well, and I think it's safe to say that she and Guy are not exactly perfect candidates to be siblings.'

'Oh, pooh. Guy and Lana got off on the wrong foot with that silly mitten experience, that's all. I'm sure they'll be close as two peas in a pod in no time at all.'

I looked at Buzz as if to say 'See?' The fact that Lana and I didn't like each other didn't even faze my mother. She just expected us to get over it so she could go on her merry way and get married to Jerry Zuckerman. But Buzz wasn't ready to give up.

'I'm not sure you understand how things are between Lana and Guy. Let's put it this way: no pod in its right mind would want to have those two peas in it at the same time,' Buzz said.

'I'm an optimist, Buzzy,' said my mom. 'I know my Guy, and when he puts his mind to something – watch out.'

'And what exactly is it that you think I'm going to put my mind to, Mom?' I asked.

'Putting your differences with Lana aside and welcoming Jerry with open arms so that we can all be one big happy family,' my mother said.

I rolled my eyes. There she went again with that one-big-happy-family stuff. Man, did that bug me. What was the matter with the family we already had – the one without Lana and Jerry Zuckerman? But there was no use in arguing. The answer was clearly to take matters into my own hands at this point and put the brakes on this marriage pronto, before it was too late.

'Let's go upstairs, Buzzard. I think there's something up there we should both put our minds to right away, if you know what I mean.'

'You boys working on a project together?' my mother asked.

'Yep,' I said, pulling Buzz out the door by his sleeve. 'A really important one that could change the world. At least mine, anyway.'

'That's nice. You're welcome to stay for dinner, Buzzy,' my mother called after us. 'We're having Mexican food. I've invited Jerry and Lana too!'

My heart stopped in my chest. Dinner with *them*?

'I am absolutely not going to eat with those—' But Buzz looked at me wide-eyed and quickly slapped his hand over my mouth before I could finish my sentence.

'That sounds positively *garbanzo*!' he called back to her. Then he started pushing me quickly up the stairs toward my room.

'What does?' I said to him as I turned around and knocked his hands off me. 'Watching me squirm while my mother and Jerry Zuckerman make goo-goo eyes at each other and Lana sits around stuffing her face with tacos and calling me names? I'm not going to eat dinner with them, and that's final.'

'You want to bust up Jerry and your mom, don't you?' he asked.

'You know I do. And fast. But what does that have to do with eating dinner with them?'

'We need to know what we're up against.'

'What do you mean?' I asked.

'How much do you know about Lana's dad? I mean, what kind of person is he? What makes him tick?'

'How am I supposed to know? I've never even met the guy.'

'Exactly. You have to meet the enemy before you can defeat the enemy,' Buzz said in a serious voice.

'Who said that?' I asked. 'Winston Churchill?'

'I'm not sure. It's possible I made it up, or it could be I'm remembering it from some old superhero show.'

He pushed past me, went on up the stairs, and headed into my room.

'What matters is it makes sense, doesn't it?'

he continued as he sat down in his usual spot at the foot of my bed. 'I mean, we have to know something about Jerry Zuckerman in order to come up with a plan for how to get rid of him, right?'

I followed him into my room.

'I guess,' I said, flopping down on the bed and kicking off my shoes. 'But what do you mean "get rid of him"? We're not going to have to hurt him, are we?'

'Sheesh, Guy. Of course not. We're not out to break any bones here – we're just going to help your mom and Jerry Zuckerman see that the two of them getting married is a really bad idea. That's all. And this dinner party tonight is a perfect opportunity to meet the enemy – that would be Mr Zuckerman, since he's the one your mom is planning to marry – and get started on figuring out how to accomplish our mission. Besides, your mom's making Mexican food, and tonight is leftovers at my house.'

'Oh, so that's what this is all about. You're in the mood for Mexican food, huh?' I said.

'How could you accuse me of being that low, Guy Wire?' said Buzz. 'Tonight is going to be the beginning of the end of the impending Zuckerman-Strang nuptials if we play our cards right. The fact that we're going to be eating Mexican food while we figure out how to do it is nothing more than a fortunate turn of fate.'

'Do you really believe all that stuff about meeting and defeating?' I asked.

'Absolutely. Every time Jerry opens his mouth, he's going to be handing us ammunition. Oh, speaking of mouths, do you want me to tell Lana to shut hers and quit calling you names if she starts in again tonight?' Buzz asked. 'I can't promise anything – you know how she can be – but every now and then she does listen to me.'

'Don't waste your energy, Buzzard. We've got bigger fish to fry.'

'Wait a second! I thought you said we were having Mexican.'

CHAPTER FIVE

My mother called up to us, 'Boys, come on down! Company's here!'

I looked at Buzz.

'Ready to meet the enemy?' he asked.

'Ready,' I said.

Lana was standing at the foot of the stairs. Buzz hopped on the banister and slid down, landing with a thump right at her feet.

'Hello, Your High-ness,' he said.

That's Buzz's nickname for Lana on account of her superiority complex and the fact that she's so tall that she's up a lot higher than the rest of us.

'Hey, Buzzer,' she said.

'Hi, Lana,' I said as I came down the stairs.

'Shut up, Girlie Guy,' she said to me.

Well, the evening was certainly off to a wonderful start. She hadn't called me that name in years, and now I'd heard it twice in the same day.

'Guysie, come meet Jerry,' my mother called from the living room.

'Yeah, *Guysie*,' Lana said snottily.

I went into the living room and got my first glimpse of Jerry Zuckerman. He was sitting in the rocking chair by the window. Something about him looked weird. For some reason his knees seemed to be right up near his armpits. I understood why as soon as he unfolded himself from the chair and stood up. And up and up. The guy was as tall and skinny as a palm tree. No wonder Lana was so big.

Buzz whistled low behind me.

'Man, what are you, like seven feet or something?' he said.

Jerry laughed. 'Last time I looked I only had two,' he said.

Buzz looked at him blankly. Jerry pointed to his feet.

'Oh, I get it,' said Buzz. 'Two feet.' And he tried to force out a polite little laugh.

'You must be Guy,' Jerry said, turning to me and sticking his huge hand out for me to shake.

'And I must be Buzz,' Buzz said, coming over and shaking hands with Jerry too.

'Oh, I think I've heard Lana speak of you, Buzz.'

'Really?' Buzz said. 'What did she tell you?'

'She mentioned that you live over on Robin Street,' he said. 'That's a very nice neighbourhood.'

'Uh-huh,' Buzz said, not doing a very good job of hiding his disappointment. I knew he was wondering if all Lana had bothered to tell her father about him was his address.

Then Jerry turned to me, and pointing to Lana, who was leaning against the door-frame with a sour look on her face, he said, 'Of course you know Lana, right, Guy?'

I nodded.

'And I remember Lana from the production of *The Princess and the Pea* way back in second grade,' my mother said, smiling brightly at Lana. 'You played the queen, right?'

Lana looked down at her feet and shrugged.

'Do you remember those crazy costumes I made for you all? What a scream!' my mother said. 'Remember, Guysie?'

I cringed. Who didn't remember the costumes my mother had made for that play? She dressed us all up in bathing caps and green boxer shorts, cotton balls and capes made out of Astroturf. Lana was supposed to walk around carrying a queen's sceptre that was made out of a toilet plunger covered with tin foil, but she refused. My mother spent the whole time going on and on about her artistic vision, and we all kept wondering if what she meant was that she was having trouble with her eyesight and that's why she couldn't tell that she'd dressed us up like a bunch of lunatics. Let's put it this way: anybody who hadn't realised that my mother was a total nutcase before then certainly knew it by the time the final curtain came down.

'I'm sorry I missed that production, Lorraine – I'm sure it was wonderful,' Jerry said to my mother. 'Unfortunately, it seems like I have to miss most of Lana's performances because of my work schedule.'

'What sort of work do you do?' Buzz asked, jumping at the first opportunity to gather some personal information about Jerry.

'I'm a bozo,' he said.

'Excuse me?' said Buzz.

'In his spare time Jerry volunteers as a clown at the local hospital – you know, cheering up sick kids,' my mother explained.

Jerry reached into his pocket and pulled out a handkerchief. He blew his nose into it with a loud honk. A really loud honk. Too loud to be real. Then I realised he was squeezing some sort of horn in his pocket every time he blew his nose. When he finally stopped, he made a big show of taking the hankie away from his face, and there was a large black plastic fly stuck to the end of his nose. He looked at it cross-eyed and pretended to be unable to coordinate his hands well enough to brush it off.

I looked at Buzz. I could tell he was thinking the same thing I was. This guy really *was* a bozo.

'What do you do when you're not being a clown, Mr Zuckerman?' Buzz said, when Jerry had finally finished his routine.

'I play in the local symphony orchestra,' Jerry said.

'What do you play?' asked Buzz.

'Out of tune,' he said, looking Buzz right in the eye.

'Huh?' said Buzz.

'Out of tune, get it?' he said, 'I play *out of tune*.' He crossed his eyes again and stuck out his tongue. The plastic fly was sitting on the tip of it.

'Jerry's a major kidder.' My mother laughed. 'Aren't you, honeybunch?'

'*General* Kidder to you, baby.' Jerry saluted and then chucked my mother playfully under the chin. She laughed again.

This guy was starting to bug me in a big way.

'Jerry plays the piccolo,' my mother said. 'You know, one of those cute little tiny flutes.'

Jerry put his hands up near his face and wiggled his fingers, pretending he was playing a ridiculously small flute. When his fingers got tangled together, he crossed his eyes again and stuck out his tongue. The plastic fly wasn't there this time, but then he curled his tongue up and touched the end of his nose with it, and the fly dropped out of his left nostril onto his tongue.

Ay-yi-yi. I stood there watching my mother laughing delightedly at her idiot clown of a boyfriend – no, worse – her idiot clown of a *fiancé* – and I wished with all my might that the floor would open up and I'd be sucked down into the earth for ever, never to have to witness something this painfully corny again.

'Who's hungry?' my mother asked cheerfully.

'I'm Jerry, but I'd be glad to give you a hand in the kitchen until Hungry shows up.'

My mother laughed, and the two of them went off to the kitchen holding hands.

I looked at Buzz. I could feel that my face was red.

'Okay, Buzzard,' I whispered. 'We've met the enemy and he's horrible. Hurry up and tell me what we do next.'

'We still need more information,' said Buzz.

'He's too tall. He plays a tiny flute. He pulls plastic flies out of his nose. He's a clown. How much more do we need to know?' I asked.

'What are you two whispering about?' Lana pushed herself off the door-frame where she'd stayed slumped and silent during all of this, and walked over to us.

'Nothing,' said Buzz.

'You're talking about my dad, aren't you?' she said.

'Maybe,' I said.

'What about him?' asked Lana.

'Nothing,' I said.

'No, really. What about him? Do you think he's weird or something?' she asked.

'Well, maybe a little,' I said.

'Ha! Look who's talking. At least he knows the difference between normal clothes and a Halloween costume. What is your mother wearing tonight anyway, a tablecloth?'

As a matter of fact, she was. She has several

skirts she's made out of tablecloths. This particular outfit is one she calls 'Picnic in the Park' because the skirt is made out of a red-and-white-checked cloth that she wears with a belt onto which she hot-glued disposable plastic silverware and a bunch of black rubber ants. A lot of her outfits have themes.

'Hey, my mother may dress funny,' I said, 'but at least she knows how to *be* funny if she wants to be. Your father probably makes those poor kids at the hospital even sicker with his stupid jokes.'

Lana made a grab for me, but Buzz got between us.

'Hey, you guys, come on,' he said. 'Knock it off.'

'I'll knock something off, all right – like your fat head, Girlie Guy.' She took a swing at me and actually came close to connecting, but I grabbed her wrist just in time to keep her from making contact.

'Hey, don't hurt her!' Buzz said, pulling my hand off of Lana's wrist.

Lana took that opportunity to pinch me hard on the arm.

'Ouch!' I yelped.

'Hey, don't hurt *him*!' Buzz said, pushing Lana away from me, 'Sheesh, you guys, what's with you?'

Lana and I glared at each other. I was rubbing my arm and she was breathing hard and wheezing a little. I wondered if she was going to have another one of her asthma attacks.

'Don't you get it?' Buzz said.

'Get what?' I said. 'That there's a wheezing psychopath standing in my living room insulting my mother and pinching me?'

'No. That you two are the *same*,' Buzz said.

'What are you talking about?' said Lana. 'I don't have one thing in common with him.'

'Yes you do, Lana. Don't you see? You both want the same thing. You don't want your parents to get married to each other.'

He was right.

'So what are you saying?' Lana asked Buzz.

'I'm saying that you guys are not each other's

enemies. You're allies. You have to bury the hatchet and work together.'

'Work together on what?' Lana asked.

'On coming up with a plan for how to convince our parents that there's no way we could ever in a million years be one big happy family if they got married,' I said.

'I'll second that,' Lana said.

'If we all three work together on this thing, I'm sure we can come up with a good plan,' Buzz said.

'Yoo-hoo! Dinner's on!' my mother called from the other room. 'Come and get it, *muchachos*!'

'So what do you say – are you willing to call a truce and work on this together?' Buzz asked.

I looked at Lana and tried to imagine how it would feel to be on the same side as her.

'I guess I'm willing if you are,' I said.

'I suppose,' she said grudgingly. 'But just so you know, I still think you're scum.'

'The feeling is *way* mutual,' I said.

'Okay then,' said Buzz happily, 'we're a team. Now let's eat.'

CHAPTER SIX

After dinner Buzz and I went upstairs. We left Lana sitting at the table drinking a cup of my mother's homemade herbal tea, which we both passed up. We'd had it before and were wise to the fact that it tasted like a cross between boiled sweat socks and lawnmower clippings.

I pulled off my sweatshirt, tossed it in the chair, and flopped down on the bed.

'That was one of the worst meals I've ever had to sit through in my life,' I said.

'You gotta admit the food was pretty good,' Buzz said.

'Yeah, but who could eat anything with that stupid plastic fly showing up all over the place? Did you see when he put it in his ear? What is the matter with that guy? Why does he think that's funny?'

'I don't know. But your mom seems to think it's funny too. She laughs every time he does it,' Buzz said.

'I know. It's scary, isn't it?'

'Well, she used to like all that wacky stuff your dad did too,' Buzz said.

'I know, but this is worse than any of the junk he pulled.'

'Worse than the oyster trick?' Buzz asked.

'That was annoying and gross, but at least it was original.'

There was a knock at the door.

'I hope it's not that clown and his pet fly,' Buzz said.

'Come in!' I called.

It was Lana. She came in holding a plate with one of my mother's lumpy white dumplings on it.

'Your mother gave me this for dessert, but she told me not to ask you what's inside it,' she said. 'So what's inside it?'

'Marmalade,' answered Buzz. 'It's like grape jelly if you're from London.'

Lana rolled her eyes, walked across the room, pulled open my window, and pitched the dumpling deep into the backyard. We heard it *thwack* against a tree.

'What?' she said, looking at our shocked faces.'It's biodegradable.'

'I wouldn't be so sure,' I said.

'Whatever,' she said, tossing my sweatshirt onto the floor and making herself comfortable in my rolling desk chair. 'So have you two geniuses come up with a plan yet? Because they're down there talking about converting the dining room into a room for me after my dad and I move in.'

'Oh man,' I said as the seriousness of the whole thing sank in a little further. 'Buzzy, we have to get moving.'

'There's no plan yet, Lana, but I'm glad you're here. I think it's probably a good idea for all three of us to be in on the initial planning session,' Buzz said.

'Translation: you two Dilly Bars are totally lost without my help.'

She pushed off the edge of the desk with her hands, lifted her feet, and spun full circle around in the chair. Buzz laughed, but I had had about all I could stand of Lana's crummy attitude.

'Hey, we could easily come up with a plan without any help from you,' I said.

'Oh, yeah?' she said, and spun around again with a snort.

'Yeah,' I said, loudly.

'Let me see, I think maybe I remember a couple of your plans, Guy, don't I? Like the one to uncover who your "true parents" were. Bob-o almost ended up getting murdered in that one, didn't he?'

'No. That was just a misunderstanding,' I said.

'What about the one where Buzz broke your foot with a can of peaches? Was that a misunderstanding too?'

'That was an accident, Lana. I explained that to you before,' Buzz said.

'Misunderstandings and accidents. Yep, those

are pretty impressive plans you've cooked up, fellas,' Lana said smugly.

'Well, maybe we should try something more your speed, like dumping hot food in your father's lap,' I said.

That was a reference to something that had happened the year before, when Lana had thought I wasn't treating Autumn the right way. Autumn asked me if I wanted to go to the movies with her and I wasn't sure at first. Since they're best friends, Lana got all bent out of shape about me making her wait for an answer, and so she dumped a plate of macaroni and cheese on me in the cafeteria.

'It worked, didn't it?' she said. 'Not that Autumn put up with you for very long. She dumped you like a load of gravel.'

'Ha! She didn't dumped me, I dumped her,' I said, jumping up.

'You guys . . .' Buzz said, trying to step in and get us to stop.

But Lana went on. 'Oh, puh-lease. Talk about rewriting history, Strang. The whole world knows Autumn traded in your pathetic carcass for that hunk Max LaMott.'

'You think Max LaMott is a hunk?' Buzz asked, sounding a little concerned.

'He's nothing but a big drama dweeb,' I said.

'Hardly. He's very talented. He's going to be a famous stage actor or a movie star some day.' Lana sniffed.

'Do you really think he's a hunk?' Buzz asked again.

'I've seen fire hydrants with more talent than he has,' I said.

'But Lana, do you really think he's a—' Buzz started to ask once more, but Lana interrupted him impatiently.

'Shut up, will you, Buzzer?' she said. 'I'm not comparing Max to *you*, I'm comparing him to *Guy*.'

'Oh, good.' Buzz smiled with a sigh of relief.

'Thanks a lot for coming to my defence. Your loyalty is overwhelming, Twinkie breath,' I said.

Buzz's cheeks turned pink. 'You know I think

you've got it all over Max LaMott, Guy Wire,' he said. 'Autumn was a fool to dump you.'

'She did not dump me!' I yelled, and stamped my foot.

'Yeah, right,' Lana said with a mean little smile, as she took another spin in my chair.

'Max LaMott is so full of it, they could fly him on a string in the Thanksgiving Day parade,' I said. 'Have you noticed how he walks around talking in an English accent even though he was born right here in Cedar Springs?'

'I think the way he speaks is totally sophisticated,' Lana said.

'Some people find a southern accent attractive,' Buzz said, looking at Lana and letting a little of his southern drawl from the old days creep back in.

'Are you having a self-esteem crisis or something?' she said to him.

'You think Max is sophisticated?' I went on. 'Try phoney.'

'What do you know?' she sneered.

'I know plenty,' I said with feeling, even though

I wasn't really sure what it was I was claiming to know.

'Okay, okay, you *guys*. Stop. Have you forgotten? We're all supposed to be on the same side. If you don't quit arguing with each other, we're never going to get anywhere,' Buzz said.

'Buzz is right,' I said. 'We don't have to like each other, Lana, but for the sake of our plan, let's try to cool out.'

Lana shrugged. 'I'm cool,' she said.

'Good,' said Buzz. 'Now let's get started.'

We sat in silence for a couple of minutes.

'Oh, this is great,' said Lana. 'Don't you two have any ideas?'

'Us? What about you? Don't *you* have any ideas?' I said.

'I've got an idea what I'd like to do to your ugly face,' she said, balling up her fist and shaking it at me.

'Cut it out!' Buzz yelled. 'Cut it out right now or I'm leaving, and you two hyenas will have to figure this out by yourselves.'

We were all quiet for a second.

'Sorry, Buzzer,' Lana said. 'We'll stop now. For real. Right, Girlie Guy?'

'Would you quit calling me that?' I said.

'Oh, get over yourself, will you? It's only a nickname. But if it makes you happier, let me rephrase that. We'll stop now. Right, *Guy*?'

I nodded.

'Okay. That's better. Now listen. I think I might have an idea,' Buzz said.

'What is it?' I asked.

'I think we should have another dinner party.'

'Are you nuts?' I said.

'What good is that going to do?' Lana asked.

'Let me finish,' he said. 'We need to have another dinner party, but this time it has to be *our* party.'

'Meaning?' Lana said.

'Meaning we're going to be the ones who plan it, and it's going to be a total disaster.'

'Why, because we don't know how to plan a dinner party?' I asked.

'No, Guy Wire, because we *do*,' he answered.

Lana and I waited for him to explain himself.

'We've got to get the four of you in one room and not let anybody leave until your parents are forced to see what a horrible mistake it would be for you to try to live under one roof together.'

'How are we going to do that?' asked Lana.

'We have to start by making a list,' he said.

'Of what?' Lana asked.

'Things your parents hate,' he said.

'What does that have to do with anything?' I asked.

'It has everything to do with everything. It's the key to the whole thing. Trust me, will you?' he said to me.

And as usual, even though I probably should have known better, I did.

CHAPTER SEVEN

'Give me some paper, will you, Guy Wire?'

I handed Buzz a notebook and a pen. He drew a line down the middle of the page. On one side he wrote 'Strang' and on the other he wrote 'Zuckerman'.

'Okay, let's start with you, Lana. What does your father hate more than anything in the world?'

'What does he hate?'

'Yeah, like, what annoys him?' Buzz said.

'Um, let's see. Every fall he goes on and on about how much he hates leaf blowers. He says the sound hurts his ears, and the whole idea of them is ecologically offensive.'

I looked at her.

'What? So he's into ecology. You wanna make something of it?'

'Calm down, Your High-ness,' said Buzz quickly, 'and continue with your list.'

'Okay. Let's see. He hates marshmallows, and oh, yeah, he really hates those fluffy little dogs, the kind that yap and chase after you when you're on a bike.'

'What's he ride, like one of those giant tricycles in the circus?' I asked.

'You know, my father could probably get you some work in the circus if you want. They're always looking for *freaks*,' she said.

'Okay, you're even, so knock it off, boys and girls. What else does your father hate?' asked Buzz as he underlined *leaf blowers*, *marshmallows*, and *little yapping dogs* in the 'Zuckerman' column.

'He hates sushi,' she said.

'What's sushi?' I asked.

'Raw fish,' she answered.

'Well, who doesn't hate that?' Buzz said. 'Give me something I can work with here.'

'I'm trying. Let me think. Oh, I know – he hates musicals. And surprise parties. And rude sounds. He really hates rude sounds.'

'Like this?' Buzz said, swallowing air and letting loose a low rumbling belch.

'Yeah,' said Lana. 'Like that.'

'It's kind of surprising that a man who likes to stick flies up his nose thinks burping is rude, don't you think?' I said.

'You know what else is kind of surprising?' Lana said coolly. 'That your mother walks around with ants glued to her clothes and nobody's tried to have her committed yet.'

Buzz laughed. 'Hey, maybe that's part of the attraction – they both have a thing for fake bugs.'

Lana and I both gave him dirty looks, and he shut up and went back to his list.

'Okay, what else can you think of that he hates?' he said.

'I can't think of anything else,' said Lana. 'Isn't that enough?'

'We could probably use more, but maybe

you'll come up with some other stuff during the week.'

'Are you sure this is going to work?' I asked.

'Positive,' he said with his usual confidence. 'Your turn now. Tell me what your mother hates, Guy.'

'She doesn't hate anything,' I said.

'Everybody hates something,' Lana said.

'Really, she doesn't hate anything,' I insisted. 'She makes a point of being tolerant. It's incredibly annoying.'

'What about liver?' asked Buzz.

'Loves it,' I replied.

'Body odour?' asked Lana.

'I don't know for sure, but when she cooks broccoli and I complain about the stink, she says she doesn't mind it because it's "natural".'

'How about professional wrestling?' asked Buzz. 'Nobody's mother likes that.'

I just looked at him. I thought he knew my mother better.

'Doesn't she hate your father?' Lana asked me.

'No, why should she?' I said.

'Well, they're divorced, aren't they?'

'Yeah, so?'

'So, my parents are divorced and they can't stand each other.'

'Guy's parents are still nice to each other,' Buzz said. 'If you didn't know, you probably wouldn't even guess they were divorced.'

Lana was quiet.

'Wait, I know something my mother hates!' I said, suddenly remembering. 'She absolutely hates the word *stupid*.'

'Are you kidding me?' said Lana.

'Nope, it's the only thing I can think of that gets under her skin.'

'That's pretty stupid, if you ask me,' she snorted.

'Don't tell *her* that,' I said.

'No. *Do* tell her that,' said Buzz. 'As many times as you can at the dinner party. She'll *hate* that.'

'When are we going to have this party?' I asked.

'The sooner the better,' said Buzz.

'How about next weekend?' suggested Lana.

We all decided that would give us enough time to plan the party. We discussed some of the details, and then I asked, 'Shall we go tell them about it now?'

'Sure,' agreed Buzz and Lana.

So down we went to invite Jerry and my mother to the dinner party to end all dinner parties. Or at least that's what we hoped.

'You want to make *us* dinner?' my mother said when we told her. 'Together? Why if that isn't the sweetest—' She stopped mid-sentence and pinched the bridge of her nose, something she always does when she's about to cry. 'You see, I knew if you just put your mind to it, Guy, you two could find a way to get along.'

Lana caught my eye and pretended to put her finger down her throat and gag.

'I think this is a swell plan,' Jerry said.

'You have no idea,' I said.

Buzz jabbed me with his elbow.

'Be subtle, will you, you gumball?' he hissed.

'Lorraine, would it be okay if we had our party here?' Lana asked in this sugary voice I couldn't believe was actually coming out of her mouth. 'Daddy's place is kind of small, and you have such a lovely home, so perfect for entertaining.'

Man, was she pouring it on thick. But whatever she was pouring, our parents were eating it up with a spoon.

'Of course we can do it here,' my mother gushed. 'Just tell me what I can do to help. Your wish is my command.'

I had warned Lana and Buzz that doing it at my house was going to mean having to deal with my mother butting in, but Buzz had made up a sappy little speech for me to give when she brought it up.

'Mom, you've slaved over the hot stove and served me up so many delicious meals over the years, I want you to promise that you won't even think about setting one foot in the kitchen on Saturday. Lana and I want to do the whole thing ourselves.'

Again my mother got all choked up. She blew her nose in her napkin and smiled.

'I will not set one foot in that kitchen, Guysie. Not even a toe. I promise,' she said, holding her hand up in what I knew from experience was the Girl Scout's honour sign, her three middle fingers up and the pinkie and thumb folded down.

'What time are you kids thinking?' Jerry asked. 'I have to work at the hospital on Saturday afternoon, but I could make it by six thirty if I come straight here. Will that be okay?'

'That should be perfect,' Buzz said.

'Are you coming too, Buzzy?' my mother asked, turning to him with a big smile. 'You know you're like one of the family around here.'

'Oh, no, Mrs Strang. I've got plans for Saturday. Big plans,' he said.

'Yeah, so it'll just be the four of us,' I said.

'All under the same roof at the same time,' Lana said.

'Like one big happy family,' Buzz added.

Jerry and my mother looked at each other

and beamed, which gave Lana another opportunity to pretend to gag herself.

'What are you kids going to cook?' my mother asked. 'You're welcome to borrow some of my recipes if you'd like. I've got some wonderful, zesty dishes. Don't I, Guysie?'

'Oh, yeah, Mom. Zesty,' I said, giving Lana a jab in the ribs. I had warned her that this would probably come up too, so she was ready to head it off at the pass.

'Don't worry about the menu, Mrs Strang. *My* mom taught me how to cook last summer when I went to stay with her in California. I've got some recipes that I've been dying to try out,' said Lana.

'Lana makes great sloppy joes. Why don't you make those for us, honey?' said Jerry.

'That's not company food, Daddy,' Lana said quickly. 'We're going to whip up something special just for you. We've got it all planned. Isn't that right, Girlie Guy?'

Buzz stomped on her foot hard.

'Ouch! I mean, right, *Guy*?' Lana said, rubbing

her foot on the back of her leg and giving Buzz a dirty look.

I smiled and nodded dumbly, since we hadn't planned anything yet and the only thing I could picture setting on the table at that moment for some reason was a large roasted turkey in a groom's outfit.

'I just think this is the sweetest idea. And it's so nice that you want to work on it together,' my mother said. Then she blew her nose again, but this time when she did it, Jerry honked his horn. They looked at each other and giggled.

'Yep, we're going to do it together, all right,' I said to myself. 'So that the four of us won't ever have to do anything together again.'

CHAPTER EIGHT

Buzz loves to be in charge. And so does Lana. Their styles are different, but the two of them get along incredibly well, considering how bossy they both are. All week long the phone kept ringing with instructions from one or the other. Lana was in charge of planning the food and Buzz was in charge of planning the activities. My job was to do whatever either one of them told me to do.

'You've got to get a leaf blower,' Buzz informed me on Tuesday afternoon.

'It's January, Buzzy. Who's got a leaf blower? Will a snowblower do?' I asked.

'No, it's got to be a leaf blower,' he said. 'The sound is more annoying, plus it's less ecological than a snowblower.'

'Whatever you say,' I said.

I managed to convince old Mrs Krantz, our next-door neighbour, to lend me her leaf blower, but I had to make up some wild story about a science experiment involving forced air in order to get her to fork it over.

I was also sent on a mission to get a couple of movie musicals at the video store for Saturday night.

'Where do you keep the musicals?' I asked the man behind the counter.

'Are you into musicals, Guy?' a soft voice said behind me.

I turned around and to my horror saw that it was Autumn Hockney. And her new dweeby squeeze, Maxwell LaMott.

'Musicals are such an artificial form of theatre, wouldn't you agree, Aut?' he said to Autumn.

Here's the thing about Max LaMott. Back in the beginning of elementary school he was a shy, skinny little bucktoothed kid with a lisp and a tendency to cry and wet his pants when things didn't go his way. That's how he earned his unfortunate nickname – Max Soggy Underpants. He was pathetic. Then in fifth grade he got braces, did speech therapy, and spent a summer at some theatre camp in Maine. Bingo! Practically overnight Max Soggy Underpants became Maxwell LaMott, child actor. He stars in all the school productions, of course, but what everybody's really impressed by is that he was in a big TV commercial last year. It's one of those sappy telephone ads that are supposed to make everybody get all weepy and run out to sign up for long-distance service so they can keep in touch with their distant relatives. He plays a kid who cries after he strikes out at his ball game, and then his grandfather calls him up and tells him about the time, way back when, when he did the same thing. There's a big close-up at the end of it with Max LaMott drying his tears and wiping his nose on his sleeve. Big deal. We'd all seen him do that a million times. The only thing missing was his wet pants. It hardly counts as acting in my book.

'I hate musicals,' I answered.

'So you're going to take one out so you can spend two hours watching a movie you don't like?' she said with a crooked little smile. Then she turned to Max and flipped her hair, something I used to think was cute but at that moment seemed silly. 'Some people are just too exhausting to try to figure out, don't you think, Max?' she said.

'Exactly,' he said, pronouncing it 'ex-ahhh-ctly.'

They left a minute later and Max actually put sunglasses on as they walked out the door even though it was grey and cloudy outside. How stuck up can you get? I watched them through the window and wondered how I ever could have had a crush on someone who could have a crush on someone as fake and full of himself as Max Soggy Underpants LaMott.

'So do you need help finding a movie?' the guy behind the counter asked.

'Yeah, which musicals have you got?' I said.

'Man, there's tons,' he said, sort of waving his arm over towards a wall of videos.

'Which one is the most annoying?' I asked.

'That's a tough question,' he said. 'If you ask me, they're all pretty annoying. I mean, right .when you're settling into the story, everybody jumps up and starts running around singing and dancing for no good reason. Personally, it makes me buggy.'

I walked over and pulled a movie off the shelf at random. I looked at the title. It was called *Seven Brides for Seven Brothers.* The picture on the front showed a bunch of western-looking guys with really big white teeth dancing around in a barnyard. The blurb on the back said that it was 'rollicking good fun'.

'Ever seen this one?' I asked.

'Nope, but it looks pretty bad, doesn't it?' he said, coming out from behind the counter to look at the box.

I nodded.

'How about this one?' I asked, holding up a copy of something called *Gigi.*

'Wait a sec,' he said, pulling a box off the shelf himself. 'How about *this* one? It's called *Paint*

Your Wagon, and it says here that it's the first and only musical starring Clint Eastwood. It's got a song in it called "I Talk to the Trees".'

'Does Clint Eastwood sing it?' I asked, looking over his shoulder at the box.

'I'm not sure. But does it really matter? Whoever sings it, with a dumb title like that, it's gotta be annoying, don't you think?'

'Yeah,' I said. 'I'll take it.'

The phone was ringing when I got home.

'Hello?' I said, grabbing it off the hook before I'd even taken off my jacket.

'I'm gonna need a mackerel for Saturday,' Lana said.

'A mackerel? As in a fish?' I said.

'Yeah, a fish. What did you think I meant, a horse?'

I took a deep breath and ignored the insult.

'Where do I get it?' I asked.

'Well, it's got to be fresh, so you'll have to go down to the market early on Saturday morning.'

'How early?'

'I don't know. Like five or something,' she said.

'Five in the *morning*?' I said. 'What are you, nuts? We're not eating until six thirty at night! Why do I have to go so early?'

'Look, if you can't handle it, I'll go myself. But it has to be done in the morning because that's when they're fresh.'

'How come you're such an expert on fish all of a sudden?' I asked.

'For your information I've been reading up on it on the Internet.'

I was going to ask her if the site was called mackerel.com when the Call Waiting beeped.

'Can you hold on a second?' I asked.

'No, just tell me – are you gonna go get the fish on Saturday morning or not?' she said.

'Yes,' I said.

'Good.'

She hung up and I picked up the other call.

'Hello?'

'We need to get a dog lined up right away,' Buzz said.

'What are you talking about?'

'We need a dog for Saturday night,' he said.

'Mrs Krantz next door's got a German Shepherd,' I said. 'She gave me the leaf blower, so I can probably get her to lend me the dog—'

'No, no, we need a little dog, remember? Something yappy and fluffy. Who do you know who's got one of those?' he asked.

'Nobody, offhand,' I said.

'You better go to the pound and borrow one then,' Buzz said.

'You can't borrow dogs from the pound! Besides, I'm already going to the fish market at five in the morning,' I said. 'Can't you find the dog?'

'Hey, what are you whining about? I'm working my butt off on this thing, and it's not even my mother who's threatening to get married,' Buzz said.

'I'm sorry. You're right. But where am I going to get a dog on such short notice, Buzz Cut?'

'I don't know, but the bottom line is we need a yipping, fluffy little dog, and it's your job to get it. If you can't borrow it from the pound, then figure out some other way to get one. It's Thursday. You've got two whole days. Just do it.'

'Okay,' I said.

We hung up. Where was I going to find an obnoxious yipping little dog to borrow? And how was I going to do it by Saturday? What was I supposed to do, ride my bike down Main Street with a mackerel strapped to my handlebars and lasso some poor old lady's miniature pooch as I rode by?

I heard the front door open and close. My mother was home.

'Honeybunch, are you home?' she called. 'Come out here and see what I picked up. You're not going to *believe* it!'

I closed my eyes and took a deep breath. What was it going to be this time? An antique plaster donkey with a broken barometer embedded in its side? A new double-barrelled glue gun? A nice white tablecloth to make her wedding dress out of? We had an attic and a garage filled to the brim with things my mother had picked up and hauled home because she just couldn't resist them. And then I heard it. An unmistakable sound.

Yip! Yip! Yip!

Could it be?

CHAPTER NINE

'Guysie, meet Sweetie Pie Dough,' my mother said, scooping the little dog up into her arms and making him wave one fuzzy white paw at me.

'Where did you get that?' I asked in amazement.

'I found him walking around in the parking lot at Peck's Supermarket.'

'Whose is it?' I asked.

'I don't know. He doesn't have any tags. I'm going to call the pound in a minute and see if anyone's reported him missing. But until we locate the owner, I couldn't see leaving him out there in the cold like that.' She put her face down near the dog's and let him lick her mouth with his little pink tongue. 'Who is Mommy's little Sweetie Pie Dough?' she asked in sickening high-pitched baby talk.

'How do you know that's his name?' I asked, wincing at the syrupy sound of her voice, not to mention the sight of that dog tongue, lapping at my mother's bright-red lipstick.

'I don't know his name. But I have to call him something. I think Sweetie Pie Dough fits him just perfectly, don't you?' She looked at the dog again and crooned, 'Who's the sweetest little pie-dough boy? Who is? Who is? Who *is*?'

The dog suddenly jumped out of her arms and started running around the room, yapping and biting at my ankles.

Perfect! I thought. *Obnoxious, small, and yappy – just what the doctor ordered.*

'Well, I guess I'd better go call the pound,' my mother said, heading for the kitchen.

'No, wait!' I said. 'Let me do it. You stay here with Sweetie Pie Dough. It looks like he may have bonded with you already, and you shouldn't leave him right now. It might be traumatic for him. I learned that in, uh, Humanities.'

At that moment the dog ran over, grabbed hold of me with his front paws, and got ready to do that nasty humpy thing dogs sometimes do to people's legs.

'Oh look, Guysie, he's bonding with you, too!' my mother said.

'Uh-huh,' I said, shaking the dog off my leg and quickly heading into the kitchen. 'I'm gonna call the pound now, Mom!' I called out to her.

'When you describe him, make sure to tell them that his back left paw has the cutest little black mark on it. And that his sweet little right ear is kind of bent, and that he seems exceptionally bright,' my mother called out to me.

'Okay!' I yelled back.

Yeah, right. Like I would tell someone that that noisy little fur ball was exceptionally bright. I picked up the phone and pretended to dial, leaving my finger on the hook so the number wouldn't go through. I had no intention of calling anyone about Sweetie Pie Dough. At least not until after Saturday night.

I went through the whole routine, even repeating my mother's description of the dog just in case she was listening, and then I hung up and went out to give her the news that no one had reported the dog missing. When I got into the living room, my mother was sitting on the couch with the dog on her lap.

'Who has the sweetest little poochy woochy facey in the whole world?' she said to him. 'You do. Oh, yes you do. Oh, yes you *do*.'

This was going to be hard to take. Then I reminded myself that what was making my stomach turn over was exactly what Jerry was going to see on Saturday. This was going to be great!

'Mom, nobody's reported him missing,' I said, trying to sound appropriately concerned.

'Well, then Sweetie Pie Dough will just have to stay right here with us, won't he?' she said, rolling his little ears up on both sides of his head so that he looked like a doggy version of George Washington.

What a stroke of luck this was! I went off to call Buzz and tell him the good news.

'I've got great news,' I said as soon as he picked up.

'Oh yeah, what?'

'I've got the dog!'

'Already?' he said.

'Yep. And not only is he small and yappy and obnoxious, my mother is so into him, I can guarantee that it's going to make Jerry completely sick,' I said.

'Perfect!'

'So what's left to do?' I said.

'I'm supposed to get marshmallows and party hats today,' said Buzz.

'What for?' I asked.

'The marshmallows are for some salad or something, and the party hats are part of the surprise.'

'What surprise?' I asked.

'Remember Lana said her dad hates surprises?'

'Yeah.'

'Well, Lana and I came up with the idea of making Saturday night a surprise birthday party for him.'

'Is it his birthday?' I asked.

'No, his birthday's not until next month. That's why he's gonna be particularly surprised. Hey, maybe we should let your mother in on the surprise part. You know how she is about birthdays.'

'Do I ever,' I said.

My mother has a way of making birthdays so excruciatingly embarrassing that you wish you'd never been born. Sometimes she puts on a play about your life in front of all your friends, or decorates a cake with you painted naked on top with tan frosting and a gumdrop for a belly button. No matter what, it's humiliating.

'Maybe we should let her make the cake,' I suggested.

'Good idea,' Buzz said. 'Ask her about it after we hang up, okay?'

This whole plan sounded like it was coming together perfectly.

'Let's meet at the Mini-Mart, pick up the junk, and then go over to Lana's for a last group planning session, okay?' Buzz said.

'Cool. I'll meet you there in ten minutes,' I said.

I asked my mother about making the cake. She loved the idea and promised to keep it a secret. She said she knew just what to make, and I knew she wouldn't disappoint. When I left, she was holding Sweetie Pie Dough under one arm while she went through a cookbook looking for a recipe for a cake that would 'hold its shape'.

'What shape are you going to make?' I asked.

'You'll see,' she said with a little smile.

'Remember, it's a surprise,' I said.

'I love surprises!'

'That's good,' I said softly to myself as I closed the door behind me and went to go meet Buzz.

CHAPTER TEN

'Hurry up, Buzzard,' I said. 'I think I hear his car pulling up.'

It was six thirty on the dot Saturday night. Lana was inside working on dinner, and Buzz and I were out in my garage trying to get the leaf blower started. The plan had been for me to be out in front making an annoying amount of noise with it when Jerry got there, but by the time we finally figured out how to work the thing, Jerry had already gone inside my house.

'Start blowing near the window anyway, and I'll sneak around back and ask Lana to find out if it's annoying him, okay?' Buzz said.

So I walked back and forth under the front windows blowing around the only two brown leaves I was able to scare up that weren't frozen solid to the ground. It was freezing outside and I'd forgotten my gloves. I wondered if I was in danger of getting frostbite. I decided it was worth it if it meant Jerry might get annoyed enough to think twice about marrying into my family.

After what seemed like forever, Buzz came back. He shook his head and drew his finger across his throat. I turned off the leaf blower.

'With the windows closed tight and the music on in there, she says you can't hear that thing at all,' he said.

My mother stuck her head out the door at that moment. Buzz quickly ducked behind a bush so she wouldn't see him.

'What in the world are you up to out there, Guysie?' she called.

'Nothing much,' I said, blowing on my numb fingertips in a vain attempt to get some feeling back in them.

'Well, come in here, will you? Poor Lana is

slaving away out in the kitchen all by herself. I thought this was supposed to be a team effort. You've got to hold up your end of it, Guy.'

I shot a look over at Buzz.

'I am holding up my end,' I said. 'Lana asked me to come out here and gather some, um, some twigs and leaves and junk for a centrepiece for the table.'

'Oh, how cute!' my mother said. 'You two are just too much.'

'Yeah, right,' I said, leaning over and picking up the two brown leaves I'd been blowing around. 'I'll be in in a minute, okay?'

She waved to me and shut the door. Buzz came out of the bushes and handed me a stick.

'What's this for?' I asked.

'Your centrepiece,' he said.

'Thanks.' I added it to the leaves and tried to close my frozen fingers around them.

'I've gotta go home for dinner now, Guy Wire, but I'll check in by phone later on, okay?' Buzz said. 'Listen, good luck. I hope it works out okay. You'd better get inside and help Lana.'

'Thanks, Buzz Cut,' I said. 'If this works, I'll owe you one. Big time.'

He took off toward his house, and I went in the back door into the kitchen.

'It's about time,' Lana said. 'The plan wasn't for me to be in here doing *everything* while you goof around outside with Buzz.'

'I wasn't goofing around. I was doing the leaf blower thing. Give me a break, will ya? I'm half frozen to death.'

'Well, it was a total waste of time. Your mother's playing Elvis in there. He didn't even hear the blower.'

'What do you want me to do, bring the thing in here and blast Sweetie Pie Dough around the room with it?' I said.

Lana took a deep breath.

'I promised Buzz that we wouldn't fight,' she said, 'so I'm going to try to stay calm, pretend that I don't think you're a total zipper head, and just ask you to help with the fish, okay? Can you handle that?'

I'd handled that mackerel about as much as I

wanted to already. I'd picked it up from the fish market at five thirty that morning and carried the package home in the dark on my bike. The road was slippery, and my bike skidded a couple of times, making me have to squeeze the fish tight under my arm in order not to drop it. The plastic bag it was wrapped in sprang a leak, and I came home stinking to high heaven.

'What are you making, anyway?' I asked.

'Sushi,' she said.

'Raw fish?'

'Yeah, my dad hates it. And I don't blame him – I mean, look at it.'

Lana had laid the raw fish on one of my mother's platters and stuck some parsley in its mouth.

'Is that the way you're supposed to serve it? Whole like that with the eyes and the guts in and everything?' I asked.

'You got a better idea?' Lana said, putting her hands on her hips.

'No. I just think it's gross, that's all.'

'It's supposed to be gross. Remember?'

'What else are we having?' I asked.

'Marshmallow salad,' she said.

'Is that all?'

'Yeah, that's all I could think of that my dad hates. And of course the only thing you came up with that your mother hates is the word *stupid.* What was I supposed to do with that – bake it in a pie? Here, you make the salad, since we're supposed to be doing this together.'

She handed me the bag of marshmallows Buzz and I had picked up at the Mini-Mart.

'What do I do with these?' I asked.

'Do I have to do everything?'

'Why are you being so snotty, Lana? All I asked was what you wanted me to do with these stupid marshmallows.'

'Why don't you just stuff a handful of them in your mouth? At least that'd shut you up for a minute. How am I supposed to think straight with you asking so many questions all the time?' Lana fumed.

'Look, at this point I'd be perfectly happy to just forget this whole dinner thing and go punch you out in front of our parents. Maybe that would be the quickest way to convince them that they're dreaming if they think you and I are ever going to get along.'

'Put them in this bowl and then pour some salad dressing over them.' Lana sighed as she handed me a large glass bowl.

'Huh?' I said.

'The marshmallows, Guy. Put them in the bowl and put dressing on them,' Lana said.

I did what she told me to do. It looked and smelled disgusting.

'Where are they now?' I asked.

'What are you, blind? They're in the bowl,' Lana said, flicking my forehead with her finger and then pointing at the soggy marshmallows.

'Not the marshmallows. I meant where are our *parents* right now?' I said.

'They're out in the living room with the dog. Why don't you get out of my hair and go check on them while I finish up in here.'

Happy for an excuse to get away from Lana, I went out to check on my mother and Jerry. The first thing I saw when I walked into the room was a pair of very large red shoes. With pom-poms on the toes. Clown shoes. Jerry had come straight from the hospital, and he was still in costume.

'Hello, Guy!' Jerry said as he stood up.

Sweetie Pie Dough growled at him and tried to nip at his cuff as he reached over the dog's head to shake my hand.

'Naughty boy,' my mother scolded as she pulled Sweetie away from Jerry's hand just in the nick of time.

Jerry looked a little tense, or at least I thought he might be tense. It was kind of hard to tell with his clown smile painted on.

'So how do you like Sweetie Pie Dough?' I asked him. 'Mom's always wanted a dog like that. She just loves those fluffy little yappers. In fact, if she had her way, we'd probably have a dozen of them running around the house, right, Mom?'

'I don't know about a dozen, but I do like this little cutie boots,' she said, squeezing Sweetie and kissing him on the nose.

Jerry flinched when he saw that.

'Do you like dogs?' I asked him.

'Well, truthfully, I'm more of a cat person, Guy. But Sweetie Pie Dough and I are trying to get to know each other,' Jerry said, tentatively reaching over to pat Sweetie's head. 'Aren't we, little fella?'

Sweetie, bless his fuzzy little heart, took that perfect opportunity to sink his sharp white teeth deep into Jerry's big hand.

'Ouch!' Jerry pulled his hand away so fast that Sweetie didn't have time to let go, and he ended up flying through the air and landing with a plop in the middle of a bowl of onion dip (with miniature marshmallows on top) that Lana had put out on the coffee table earlier.

'I know you don't particularly care for dogs, Jerry, but is it really necessary to get violent about it?' my mother said, getting up and going over to fish Sweetie out of the dip.

'I didn't do it on purpose, for heaven's sake. The animal *bit* me, Lorraine,' Jerry said.

'That big mean man doesn't like Mommy's

little Sweetie very much, does he?' my mother crooned softly to her soggy pet.

'I think it's quite the other way around,' Jerry grumbled. 'I didn't bite *him*, in case you didn't notice.'

Oh, yeah. He was tense all right.

'If you provoke an animal, you can't blame it for defending itself,' my mother said.

And she sounded just as tense as he did. This was looking pretty darned good if you asked me.

'I better go help Lana,' I said, anxious to get out to the kitchen and give Lana a progress report.

'The dog just bit your dad, and they don't seem like they're getting along that well at all,' I told her after I'd closed the kitchen door behind me.

'Who, my dad and the dog or my dad and your mom?' she asked.

'Actually, nobody seems very happy. Your dad and my mom were almost sort of having a fight,' I said.

'Great! Let's keep the ball rolling and put dinner on the table right away.'

'Okay,' I said.

'Dinner is served!' Lana called out to them as she carried the platter out into the dining room and set it on the table.

'Oh, I almost forgot,' I said, and hurried back into the kitchen.

I came back with the twig and the two dead brown leaves. I'd stuck them in a chipped coffee mug, which I plunked down in the middle of the table. It looked awful.

'What is that?' she asked.

'The perfect centrepiece for a disastrous dinner party.'

Lana held out her hand, palm up, and I slapped her five. Maybe we weren't such a bad team after all. Now that the plan was working, I was actually even starting to have fun.

'I'm sorry I said that before about wanting to punch you out,' I said suddenly.

'It's okay, Guy. I would have punched you out first anyway,' she said.

'Probably.' I laughed.

'You know, I'm starting to think this plan might actually work,' she said. 'I have a feeling dinner is gonna be great.'

'You mean it's gonna be *awful*,' I said with a huge grin.

CHAPTER ELEVEN

Dinner was delayed for a bit while my mother washed Sweetie Pie Dough off in the bathroom sink upstairs. She dried him with her hair dryer and finally sat down at the table with him in her lap. His fur was so fluffed up from the bath that you couldn't see his face any more – except for when he bared his teeth, which he did every time Jerry opened his mouth to speak.

'Well, Lana, this is a very interesting-looking dish you've made tonight,' my mother said, looking at the mackerel on the platter. 'What do you call it?'

'Raw fish,' I said.

'Sushi,' corrected Lana.

'Sushi?' said Jerry, his voice filled with dread.

'You love sushi, don't you, Dad? You told me that once. Remember?'

'Um, really? I don't know why I would have – uh, did I?' he stammered.

'I've never seen sushi served quite like this, Lana. Did your mother give you this recipe?' my mother said.

'No. This is my own personal recipe,' Lana said.

'Are you sure it's safe?' my mother asked gently.

'Now, Lorraine, I don't think Lana would serve anything that wasn't safe to eat, would you, honey?' said Jerry.

'Of course not, Daddy. How could she even think that?' Lana said, giving my mother a hurt look. 'And why was she asking if it was Mom's recipe? Was that supposed to be a diss? 'Cause Mom is a very good cook.'

'Yes, honey, she was, I mean, *is*,' said Jerry uncomfortably.

'I didn't mean to offend anybody,' my mother said quietly. 'I'm sure your mother is a fine cook,

Lana. I've just never seen sushi that looks back at you, is all.'

'It's fresh, if that's what you're worried about, Mom,' I said. 'I got it myself at the fish market this morning. Brought it home on my bike, under my arm.'

'I know, Guysie. I washed your jacket this afternoon. Twice.'

'So would you like a piece, Lorraine?' Lana said, 'It's mackerel. Supposed to be one of the fishiest fish around.'

'That's quite a claim to fame,' my mother said.

She swallowed hard and held her plate out to Lana. Lana took the knife and hacked off a piece of fish that included the head, eyeballs and all.

'There you go,' she said. 'You know, Guy and I were talking, and we think that we should make dinner together all the time after you guys get married. We could have sushi twice a week. Right, Guy?'

I nodded.

'How about you, Daddy? Want some?' Lana asked sweetly.

'Actually, I had a late lunch at the hospital, honey,' Jerry said.

'Well, maybe you'd just like some of Guy's special marshmallow salad then,' Lana said, handing him the bowl of oily marshmallows.

'I've never seen you make that salad before, Guy,' my mother said, looking into the bowl.

I shrugged my shoulders and smiled. 'Well, now you have, Are you going to have some?' I asked, turning to Jerry.

'I . . . I . . . don't know quite what to say,' Jerry began. 'I mean, I know you kids must have worked very hard on this meal, but I think you forgot somehow, Lana, that I don't care for marshmallows. Or sushi. At all.'

Lana gave me a quick look and then launched into the most realistic crying fit I've ever seen anyone fake. Big tears rolled down her cheeks, and she blubbered and whimpered as she spoke, all the while making sure to use the word *stupid* as many times as possible. It was a very impressive show.

'I guess this dinner was all just a stupid idea. I

told you it was stupid, Guy. The whole thing is stupid. Why would anyone want to eat this dinner? Your mother doesn't even think it's safe. She acts like I'm trying to poison her or something. She hates me. And I'm so stupid not to remember you don't like sushi, Daddy. Stupid, stupid, stupid. And you're stupid too, Guy Strang. I told you I wasn't sure if my dad liked marshmallows, but you insisted, yes, you practically *forced* me to let you make your stupid marshmallow salad. Now look at the mess we're in. All this hard work and planning and I'll bet even that stupid little dog wouldn't want to eat this.'

'I'm sure my Guy wouldn't have *forced* his marshmallow salad on you, Lana,' my mother said. 'And I don't hate you or think that you're trying to poison me. I do wish you wouldn't call my dog stupid – I really dislike that word, and besides, Sweetie Pie Dough is an exceptionally bright—'

Jerry interrupted her at that point.

'Whether that silly dog of yours is stupid or

not is not the point, Lorraine. Can't you see that Lana needs some support here?'

'Hey, you're the one who won't eat the dinner she made, not me,' my mother said, stabbing a dripping marshmallow soaked in orange French dressing and shoving it in her mouth. You could tell it tasted repulsive to her, but she was way too mad to admit it and spit it out.

'Stupid, stupid, stupid,' Lana wailed, squeezing out some fat fresh tears. Boy, this girl was good.

'Lana, sweetie, you're being too hard on yourself,' Jerry said. 'Please, calm down. It's not a good idea for you to get all worked up like this. Remember your asthma. There's nothing wrong with this dinner. It's lovely, isn't it, Lorraine?'

My mother hadn't managed to swallow the marshmallow yet, and from the look on her face I wasn't sure she was going to be able to pull it off.

'Lorraine?' he said again in a not-very-nice tone of voice. 'Tell Lana the dinner is lovely.'

My mother closed her eyes and choked down the marshmallow. Then she reached for her glass and gulped down a lot of water. She wiped her mouth and glared at Jerry.

'The dinner is *lovely*, Lana,' she said, the words coming out so sharply, it sounded like she was spitting nails.

Jerry nodded in agreement and looked over at Lana. 'See? There's nothing to cry about. You know something, honey, I think it's probably high time I learned to like sushi. I'm sure I can if I try,' Jerry went on. 'Dry those tears now and give me a piece of fish. Please?'

'Yes, Lana, stop crying already and give your father a great big piece of raw fish, why don't you?' my mother said, while Sweetie growled in her lap and pulled back his little lips to show Jerry his teeth again.

'There's no need to use that tone of voice with my daughter,' Jerry said.

The sight of Jerry in his clown face and baggy polka-dot suit pleading with his bawling daughter to give him a piece of raw fish while my mother steamed and her obnoxious dog growled in her arms seemed almost too good to be true. Man, was this working. They hated each other, And clearly my mother wasn't too wild about Lana. If I could only get on Jerry's nerves like that, then the circle would be complete.

Just then the phone rang. I ran and answered it. It was Buzz.

'How's it going?' he asked.

'Like a dream!' I said.

'Spill!' said Buzz.

'Well, so far the dog bit Jerry, so he threw him in the dip, which ticked my mother off big time. Now we're in the middle of dinner, which is so disgusting no one can eat it, and Lana is crying and saying *stupid* more times than I've ever heard anyone say it before.'

'Lana's crying?' Buzz sounded worried.

'Calm down, lover boy, she's faking it.'

'Oh, okay. Good. Sounds like everything is going according to plan. But the reason I'm calling is that we forgot something,' Buzz said.

'What? We're going to watch the musical after dinner right before the surprise party. What else is there?'

'Can you belch?' Buzz asked.

'Huh?' I said. 'Oh, right. He hates rude noises. Your timing is perfect. I need something to make Jerry annoyed with me.'

'Good. Belch. Can you do it?'

'Yeah, I think so.' I swallowed a mouthful of air and tried to force it back out.

'What was that?' Buzz said. 'I didn't hear anything.'

'Wait a sec. Let me try again.'

Again I swallowed air and tried to force it out. Nothing.

'Do you want me to come over there and do it for you? You could stand by the window and I could belch for you from outside.'

'I don't think there's going to be time, Buzzard. Besides, how would I explain having to open the window? It's freezing outside.'

'Try once more,' he said.

I swallowed air again but nothing came back out.

'Look,' I said, 'we probably don't even need the belching. Things are pretty bad as they are.

And there's still the video and the surprise party.'

'Are you sure?' asked Buzz. 'I'm happy to ride over there.'

'No. But thanks for the offer. I think I should get back in there now though, okay?'

I hung up and rejoined the dinner party. Lana was still snuffling, and Jerry was trying to get up the nerve to stick a piece of raw mackerel in his mouth. When he finally started to raise the fork to his lips, Sweetie leaped out of my mother's lap and sank his teeth into Jerry's arm. This time Sweetie got a better grip. Even when Jerry waved his arm around wildly, Sweetie didn't let go. He hung from the sleeve, shaking his head back and forth and growling until finally Jerry's sleeve tore and Sweetie, with a large piece of clown suit clamped tightly between his teeth, flew across the table and landed in the bowl of marshmallow salad.

'Oh, great,' my mother said. 'Now I have to bathe him all over again.'

'I'm bleeding, Lorraine, and all you can worry about is that stupid dog.'

'He is not stupid!' my mother yelled.

Lana looked at me and winked.

'Calm down, everybody,' I said, taking charge. 'I don't think anybody's really in the mood for fish tonight. Lana, why don't you clear the table while I go clean off Sweetie Pie Dough. Jerry, there's a video in the recorder. Why don't you relax and watch that while Mom goes out in the kitchen to get the *you-know-what* ready. Okay?'

'What *you-know-what* in the kitchen?' asked Jerry warily.

'Nothing, Daddy,' said Lana. 'Just go watch the movie, okay?'

I took the dog from my mother and headed up to the bathroom with him.

'Use the good shampoo on him, Guysie. He's got very sensitive skin,' my mother called after me.

'He's not the only one,' groused Jerry, examining his arm as he headed out to the living room.

I was so grateful to the dog for all the misery he'd caused that evening that I would have washed him in perfume if that's what my mother had wanted. Sweetie cooperated, and I was back downstairs with him in ten minutes. My mom and Lana were still out in the kitchen, and Jerry was sitting on the couch talking on his cell phone and dabbing at his arm with a napkin. The video was playing in the background.

'So you're sure just rubbing alcohol is enough? . . . Uh-huh . . . Okay . . . Okay then. Thank you, Dr Matteson.'

He hung up and clipped the phone back onto his belt.

'How's the movie?' I asked. 'The guy at the video store said this was a really great one.'

'I'm not a big fan of musicals,' Jerry said.

'Really? Mom and I watch them all the time. *All* the time. Look! That's Clint Eastwood, and I have a feeling he's about to break into a song. I sure hope it's the one about talking to the trees. I just love this kind of stuff, don't you?'

'About as much as sushi and marshmallows,' Jerry said quietly.

He was the saddest-looking clown I'd ever

seen. And it was about to get worse. The door to the kitchen flew open at that point, and Lana and my mother came out wearing party hats and carrying a cake that looked like a giant red cannonball.

'Surprise!' Lana shouted.

'What the—' Jerry's mouth dropped open in horror. 'But it's not my birthday.'

'Don't you like it?' Lana said, and she made like she was going to start crying again. 'I guess it was just another stupid idea. Stupid, stupid, stupid.'

'It's not stupid, Lana,' Jerry said, standing up and coming into the dining room. He put his arm around her. 'It's just, it's just . . . well, I thought you knew that I don't like surprises.'

My mother, whose mouth was nothing more than a thin, angry red line by now, slammed the cake down on the table.

'Happy birthday,' she spat through her teeth. 'This cake, in case you can't tell, is supposed to be your clown nose.'

Jerry sat down at the table in front of his cake.

'Make a wish and blow your nose, Jerry,' my mother said.

I started to laugh at her joke, but instead something fortuitous happened. All that air I'd swallowed on the phone with Buzz earlier gathered force and chose that perfect moment to come blasting out in one of the most magnificent rumbling belches the world has ever known. It went on and on, and when at last it died out, the room was completely silent for a minute.

'Awesome,' Lana whispered to me.

'Excuse me,' I said.

'My goodness, Guysie,' my mother giggled. 'That was impressive. Are you okay, honey?'

'No, he is *not* okay,' Jerry said, slapping his napkin down on the table and raising his voice. 'What he is is unbelievably rude. I have never seen anything like it. It's bad enough that you allow that vicious little mongrel of yours to sit at the table with us, but now this is just too much. Don't you people care one whit about manners around here?'

It was like standing at the foot of a volcano, feeling the earth tremble beneath my feet as the thing began to blow.

'You have some nerve, Jerry Zuckerman,' my mother began slowly. 'We *people* have been sitting here at this table trying to choke down a hunk of disgusting raw mackerel while having to stomach your whining, manipulative daughter insulting my dog and blaming my son for a lousy menu plan I'm sure he had nothing to do with. I have tried my level best to ignore the fact that you have flung my pet not once, but twice, into bowls of food, all the while wearing a ridiculous clown suit. But now, finally, I believe *you* people have located the straw that will break even this tolerant old camel's back. My dog is not stupid. Do you hear me? And what's more, my Guy is not rude.'

Jerry stood up.

'I think we should get going, Lana,' he said. 'We clearly don't belong here, and I'm inclined to believe we never will.'

'No kidding,' my mother muttered loud enough for everyone to hear.

Talk about a home run. Lana looked at me, and through the shimmer of what was left of her phoney tears I could see the glimmer of triumph. We had succeeded. What a team! I could have just hugged her – well, in theory, anyway.

'Goodbye, Jerry,' my mother said as they walked out the door.

'Goodbye, Lorraine,' he said without turning around.

And even though we didn't say it, I knew Lana and I were both thinking the same thing . . .

For ever.

CHAPTER TWELVE

'So am I brilliant or what?' Buzz said when I called him and told him the news after Lana and Jerry had left.

'You're brilliant, all right. You wouldn't have believed how well it went.'

'Yeah, and Lana doubted our ability to come up with a plan. Ha! No accidents or mistakes this time around.'

'Nope. This one played out smooth as butter. Listen, my mom already went up to bed and I'm zonked. Why don't you come over in the morning and I'll fill you in on all the gory details.'

'Okay, see you in the morning,' Buzz said, and we hung up.

* * *

'We are the master planners!' Buzz said when he showed up at my house the following morning.

'Yes, we are,' I said.

'Your mom up?'

'I don't know. She hasn't come downstairs yet.'

'I thought Sunday was pancakes-for-breakfast day,' he said. 'I was kind of counting on a big stack to celebrate our victory.'

'Yeah, well, like I said, I haven't seen her. She's probably sleeping in.'

'Where's the dog?' Buzz asked. 'I want to shake his fuzzy little paw. Sounds like he was a killer last night.'

'I haven't seen him this morning either,' I said. 'Maybe I'd better go check upstairs.'

'Want me to come?' asked Buzz.

'No, why don't you go get some juice or something in the kitchen and wait down here for me. I'll be back in a second.'

I went up the stairs and down the hall to my mom's room. The door was closed. I knocked but there was no answer. I pressed my ear up against the door, and I could hear her crying.

'Mom?' I said, turning the handle and opening the door a crack. 'Can I come in, Mom?'

'Yeah, Guysie, you can come in.' She sniffled.

She was still in bed. Sweetie Pie Dough was sitting on her pillow licking tears off her face. She looked awful. She'd gone to bed in the clothes she'd been wearing the night before. Her hair was all messed up and her eye make-up had run down her cheeks, making her look like she was wearing black war paint or something.

'Mom, are you okay?' I asked. I'd never seen her looking quite like this.

'Oh sure. I'm fine,' she said.

'You don't look fine,' I said. 'You look awful.'

That made her start crying again.

'I'm sorry, Mom. I didn't mean that the way it sounded. You look great, it's just that you look, well, awfully upset.'

'I am upset,' she said. 'Heartbroken, actually. How could I be so *stupid*?'

This was alarming. My mother never used that

word. Well, she had the night before, but that was different.

'Why do you think you're stupid?' I asked.

'How could I think that this was going to work out for Jerry and me? The only people who got along last night were you and Lana. What a joke. We thought you two were the ones who were going to have the problem, but in fact it's us. We're completely wrong for each other. How could I not have seen it? Oh, how could I have been so stupid?'

'Stop saying that, Mom,' I said, sitting down on the bed and handing her some tissues from the box on the nightstand. 'You're not stupid.'

I felt horrible. She was so unhappy. And it was all because of me. She was lying there crying her eyes out because she thought she and Jerry didn't get along. But they'd been getting along just fine until Lana and Buzz and I started messing around with them. I don't know why I hadn't anticipated this reaction. I guess I was so caught up in the plan that I hadn't thought about how my mother would feel when she and Jerry called it quits. I think maybe I thought that when she saw how mismatched we all were, she'd be relieved, even glad to have found out before it was too late. Man, was I off. She wasn't relieved, she was *heartbroken.*

'Mom. Mom. Maybe it's not as bad as you think,' I said.

'Yes it is, Guysie,' she said. 'I thought we had so much in common. After last night I feel like I don't even know the man. How could I have missed all the signs?'

She started crying much harder then. So hard she couldn't talk. Sweetie Pie Dough tried to keep up with her tears, licking away like crazy, but he finally gave up after a minute, curled up next to her, and whimpered. I felt terrible.

'Hey, Guy,' Buzz whispered from the doorway. 'Is everything okay in there?'

I got off the bed and went out in the hall, closing the door behind me.

'What's going on?' he asked.

'My mom is crying,' I said.

'For real?'

'Yeah, for real. She's not like Lana. When she cries like this, she means it. And believe me, the way she's crying right now, she *really* means it.'

'Is she crying about last night?' Buzz asked.

'Yeah. I don't know what to do,' I said. 'I think we might have gone too far.'

'What do you mean?' asked Buzz.

'Remember how you said nobody was going to get hurt? Well, I think you were wrong about that. She says her heart is broken, and you know whose fault that is, don't you?'

'Wait a second. Hearts don't actually break, Guy. That's just some expression,' Buzz said.

'Listen to her. Hear the way she's crying? That's not just some expression. She's all broken up, Buzzard. And we did it to her.'

Buzz listened outside the door for a second, then turned to me. His face was pale. 'What do we do now?' he asked anxiously.

The phone rang, and I went to get it. It was my dad. He'd got back from Spain late the night before, but because of the jet lag he was up and raring to go. He wondered if I wanted to go sledding with him on the big hill behind the high school.

'Normally that would sound great, Dad. But there's nothing normal about what's going on over here right now.'

'What do you mean?' he asked.

'Something's happened and I need to . . . well . . . something's wrong with Mom, and I think I'd better . . . Listen, Dad, could you come over here right away? I need your help.'

'I'll be right there,' he said.

CHAPTER THIRTEEN

My dad walked in the door five minutes later, hugged me tight, and then asked, 'What's going on? Is your mother okay? Is she sick or something?'

'No, Dad, she's not sick exactly.'

'Guy thinks maybe we broke her heart, Mr Strang,' Buzz said from behind me.

'Oh, hello, Buzzy, I didn't see you there. What do you mean, you might have broken her heart? How?'

'Let's go in the kitchen and sit down,' I said.

'Uh, you might want to sit in the living room instead,' said Buzz.

'Why? What's the matter with the kitchen?' I asked.

'Well, nobody cleaned up from dinner last night, and it smells pretty rank in there at the moment. Also, there's something huge and red on a plate sitting on the counter, and there are ants crawling all over it.'

'Oh man, that's Jerry's nose,' I said.

'What?!' said my father with alarm.

'Let's go in the living room, Dad, and we'll fill you in.'

We sat in the living room, and Buzz and I told my dad what we'd done. 'I guess we didn't think the plan all the way through, Dad. We were just trying to break them up so we wouldn't all have to live together. I didn't mean to hurt Mom. Honest.'

'I know, Guychick, I know. But you three managed to make a pretty big mess of things, that's for sure.'

'Do you think it can be fixed?' I asked.

'Is a broken heart for ever?' asked Buzz.

My father smiled at him.

'You could probably write a country-western song with that title and make a mint, Buzzy.'

'What should we do, Dad?' I asked.

'You need to tell her the truth,' he said.

'She's gonna kill me,' I said.

'Who's gonna kill you?' asked my mother, coming into the room.

She'd come down the stairs without our noticing and must have overheard me say that. She was still wearing her rumpled clothes, but she'd washed the mascara off her face, so she looked a little better. Sweetie Pie Dough was tucked under her arm.

'*Buenos días*, Lorraine,' my father said.

'William? What in the world are you doing here so early? I thought you were still in Spain.'

'I got back last night, and Guy asked me to come over here this morning to help out with a little problem he's having.'

'Guy has a problem?' she asked.

'Yeah, Mom, I do. Jerry didn't break your heart last night. I did.'

'What on earth are you talking about?' my mother said.

Just then the doorbell rang.

Buzz went to answer it and returned a second later with Lana and Jerry. Jerry's clown make-up was all rubbed off but he was still in his suit, which was wrinkled in the same way my mother's clothes were, like he'd slept in it. The second Sweetie Pie Dough saw Jerry, he began to growl.

'Lorraine, we need to talk,' he said.

My father stood up.

'You must be Jerry,' he said, sticking out his hand to shake Jerry's. 'I'm Guy's father, William.'

'Pleasure to meet you,' said Jerry. 'Gosh, this is a little awkward.'

He tried to smooth down the front of his clown suit and hide the torn sleeve Sweetie had ripped the night before. But there was no getting around it. He was a mess. Sweetie Pie Dough barked and growled at him again.

'I don't think that dog likes you much, Jerry,' my father said, looking at Sweetie, who was struggling to get out from under my mother's arm.

'I'm afraid he's not the only one,' said Jerry, looking sheepishly at my mother.

'Listen, Jerry,' my father said, 'may I have a word with you in private, please?'

My dad took Jerry by the elbow and led him out into the hall. A few minutes later they came back in, and my father walked over to my mother and reached for the dog.

'Be careful!' I shouted, running over to protect my father in case Sweetie tried to bite him. But it wasn't necessary. Sweetie leaped from my mother's arms right into my father's and began licking his face and wagging his ridiculous little tail.

'I'll be darned,' Jerry said.

'He likes you!' I said.

'Apparently,' my father said, patting the dog on the head. 'Unless it's just the liver-flavoured toothpaste I brushed with this morning. Drives the puppies wild.'

My mother smiled at my dad.

'Now I want you three kids to come with me,' my dad said. 'Out to the kitchen, where I understand there's a nose that needs attention. Besides, I think these two could use some privacy.' He indicated my mother and Jerry. Lana and Buzz headed toward the kitchen. I hesitated, next to my father.

'But Mom, I need to tell you what happened. It's all my fault. You think that you and Jerry don't like each other, but you do. And Lana and I, we don't really get along. In fact, basically I can't stand her,' I said.

'I heard that, Girlie Guy,' Lana shouted from the other room.

'You're just mixed up about it all because we messed with you,' I blurted out.

'Not now, Guy. Let Jerry handle it. You can talk to your mom later,' my dad said.

'But Dad—'

'But nothing. Let them handle this. You'll talk later.'

'Will somebody please tell me what's going on?' my mother asked.

My father grabbed my arm and pulled me toward the kitchen. As we left the room, I heard

Jerry say to my mother, 'I was heartbroken last night, you know that, Lorraine? Absolutely heartbroken.'

Oh, great. So we'd done it to *both* of them.

CHAPTER FOURTEEN

'P.U.,' said my father as soon as we went into the kitchen. 'It smells like there's a beached whale in here.'

'It's the mackerel,' said Lana. 'It smells even worse than it did last night.'

'What should we do with it?' asked Buzz.

'Bury it,' said my father.

'Where?' I asked.

'I don't know. Maybe behind the garage.'

'But the ground's frozen,' I said.

'Good point. Maybe we'd better put it down the garbage disposal instead,' said my dad.

'The whole thing?' asked Buzz.

'Sure. Let's try it and see what happens.'

My father picked the fish up off the platter

and stuck it into the disposal in the sink. It was so long, the tail stuck way up in the air. He turned on the water full force.

'Okay, Buzzy. Let 'er rip!' he cried, and Buzz flipped the switch on the wall.

The fish began to spin wildly as the blades noisily ground it up and slowly pulled it down into the drain. The tail flipped back and forth, making it almost look alive.

Sweetie Pie Dough barked and ran around in circles, excited by all the commotion.

'Wow!' shouted Buzz over the noise. 'That's awesome.'

We watched until it had completely disappeared. After a minute or two my father turned off the water.

'Should we do the same thing with the nose?' Buzz asked him.

'Let me see that thing,' he said.

We all leaned over the cake plate and examined the nose. Ants were all over it, and a small moving black trail of them led from the plate, down the cabinets, and along the floor to a tiny crack underneath the back door. They'd carved little tunnels into the frosting and kept disappearing inside, returning with chunks of yellow cake held high over their heads in their little pincers like trophies.

'Pretty amazing, huh?' my father said. 'Like a giant ant farm. Only red. And frosted.'

Buzz and my father were completely engrossed in watching the ants, but I was too worried about what was going on in the living room to care about bugs, and I could tell Lana was worried too.

'What do you think they're talking about in there?' I asked her.

'I don't know, but my dad didn't ever go to bed last night. He was sitting in the living room still in his clown suit when I got up this morning.'

'Same with my mom,' I said. 'I mean, she slept in her clothes too, not a clown suit.'

'Did you tell her what we did? About the plan?' she asked me.

'Not yet. I only told my dad. What about you – did you tell your dad?'

She shook her head.

'When I got up, he was just leaving to come over here, and I thought I should come along, just in case it got ugly.'

'I wonder if it's getting ugly right now,' I said, cocking my head toward the door. 'I don't hear any yelling.'

'Maybe that's because they're so mad they're not even speaking to each other,' Lana said.

'I think we should go in there and confess everything. Explain to them what we did. Doesn't that seem like the right thing to do? I mean, I didn't want them to get married, but if I'd had any idea how bad my mom would feel when they broke up, I never would have done this. I didn't want to wreck her life, just her wedding plans.'

'I know exactly what you mean. No offence, but I didn't think there was anything that could possibly be worse than ending up being related to you, Guy. But the look in my father's eyes this morning was definitely worse.'

'Can I ask you a question?' I said. 'If we could

figure out some way to get them back together, would you be willing to do it?'

'I don't know. Would *you*?' she asked.

'Yeah,' I said. 'Yeah, I think I would. I mean, I really don't want them to get married, and even though you're not quite as bad as I thought you were, I still don't want to be your brother. But I don't think I can stand the guilt of knowing that it was us who broke them up.'

'I feel the same way,' Lana said. 'But you do realise that if we go in there now and manage to undo what we did last night, we're basically handing them back those two words, *I do*, and then we're right back where we started.'

'Maybe. But maybe not,' I said, as something promising dawned on me. 'Isn't it possible that even after we tell them that we set them up last night, they'll still feel that because of what happened, they shouldn't get married?'

'I guess so. I mean, it's not like we lied to them about us not being one-big-happy-family material. It's true, we're not. All we did last night was point it out to them,' Lana said.

'Right,' I agreed. 'Hey, you know what this sort of reminds me of? One of those TV courtroom shows when the lawyer gets up in front of the jury and blabs all this incriminating stuff he's not supposed to tell them about the defendant. The judge gets bent out of shape and tells the jury that they have to "disregard those statements and it's stricken from the record" and stuff like that. Then the lawyer apologises to the court but secretly he's happy because he knows there's no way the jury is going to be able to forget what they heard. And sure enough, they end up convicting the guy, and the blabbing lawyer wins the case.'

'You lost me,' she said. 'Who's the blabbing lawyer in our case?'

'Don't you see? *We're* the blabbing lawyer. We made up this kind of sneaky plan to make sure our parents saw just how incompatible we all are, and now all we have to do is apologise to the court for being sneaky, sit back, and wait for the jury to convict.'

'Who's the jury?' Lana asked.

'*They* are!' I said. 'Don't you get it?'

'I'm not sure. So if they're the jury, who's the court?' she asked scratching her head.

'Forget it. Don't you watch TV? Look, all I'm saying is if we apologise to our parents, the worst they can do is punish us. But in the end we still win. Because there's no way they're going to be able to forget what they saw last night.'

'Oh, now I see what you're saying. Hey, that's not bad,' she said. 'For a little dweeb you're pretty smart sometimes.'

'Anybody ever tell you you've got a way with compliments?' I said.

'Come on, let's go talk to them,' Lana said, standing up and heading for the door.

'I'm right behind you.'

'Hold on a second, you two,' my father called out to us. 'Where exactly do you think you're going?'

'To apologise to the court – I mean, to talk to Mom and Jerry,' I said.

'I told you to give them their privacy right

now. You'll get your turn to explain yourselves soon enough,' he said.

'I want my dad to know about the plan,' said Lana.

'He already knows,' my father said.

'He does?' said Lana. 'How?'

'I told him. Out in the hall.'

'You *did*? What did he say? Was he mad?' Lana asked.

'I think I'll leave it to him to tell you how he feels about what you kids did,' he said. 'Right now I want you to help finish cleaning up the rest of the mess in here. When they're ready to talk to you, I'm sure they'll come get you.'

'But Dad—' I started.

'But nothing,' he said, handing me a dirty dish off the counter and pointing to the sink.

I felt kind of excited and jittery as Lana and Buzz and I rinsed the dishes and put them in the dishwasher. Lana kept the tap running so that my father wouldn't hear as she quietly explained to Buzz about my courtroom theory.

'Not too shabby, Strang. I guess all those *Perry*

Mason reruns on the Fun Channel have paid off, huh?'

By the time we'd finished with the dishes, all three of us were pretty confident that when all was said and done, victory would be ours.

'There's no way they'll get married now that they've seen how incompatible we all are. No way,' I reassured myself as I wiped down the counter.

My father had been sitting at the table the whole time with a pile of peanut butter crackers in front of him, patiently trying to teach Sweetie Pie Dough a new trick.

'Play dead, Sweetie,' he kept saying as he gently pushed Sweetie over onto his back and pulled his feet straight up into the air. Every time Sweetie cooperated, my dad gave him a cracker. Apparently my mother was right about Sweetie being no dummy, because by the time the crackers ran out, he had that trick down pat.

'Play dead, Sweetie,' my dad said again, and the dog rolled over on his back without any help and stuck his paws up, just as my mother and Jerry walked into the kitchen.

'Oh my God!' my mother screamed as she raced across the room to the dog. 'What's the matter with him? Did he faint? He's very sensitive.'

'Calm down, Lorraine. He's just showing off his new trick.' My father laughed as Sweetie jumped up and began to lick her face. She picked him up and hugged him tight. Then Sweetie caught sight of Jerry, bared his sharp little teeth, and started to growl.

'Knock that off, you naughty boy,' she said firmly, and handed him back to my father. 'William, Jerry and I need to pow-wow with the three masterminds here. I'd invite you to sit in on it, but Jerry and the dog have to be kept apart for obvious reasons, so would you be willing to watch Sweetie for a while?'

'With pleasure. How about I take him out for a walk?' said my father.

'Oh, that would be wonderful! You're such a doll, Wuckums,' my mother said, and she went to get the leash she'd made out of an old skipping rope we'd had lying around.

Wuckums has been my father's nickname for years, but it had been a while since I'd heard my mom call him that. I liked it when she did.

'Boy, your parents sure get along well, considering they're divorced,' Lana said to me. 'My mother likes my dad even less than Sweetie does.'

'Really?' I said.

'Why do you think she lives in California instead of here?'

Suddenly I felt bad for her. Seems to me like her mother ought to have stuck around even if she hated Jerry, just so she could be near Lana.

'Come on, tiger,' my father said as he pulled on his jacket and took Sweetie outside.

'Okay, you three. Let's talk turkey,' my mother said to Buzz and Lana and me.

We followed my mother and Jerry single file out to the living room, where we sat down on the couch in a row – first me, then Buzz, then Lana. Jerry sat down in the over-stuffed chair next to the couch, and my mother perched on the arm of it.

'The cat's out of the bag and we know all about what you were up to last night at the dinner party. You little devils,' she said, shaking her head. 'I must say, you did an impressive job of pulling the wool over our eyes.'

I knew what had to be done, so I jumped right in.

'I want to sincerely apologise for what we did,' I said. 'I know it was wrong and I'm sorry.'

'And me too, Dad. I'm sorry also,' said Lana quickly.

'And I'm probably the most sorry of all, because it was all my idea in the first place,' added Buzz.

That was step one. Done. Easy enough. We'd apologised to the court.

'Now I have something I want to say—' my mother said.

I knew what was coming, so I jumped right in again. 'You want to tell us about our punishments, right?' I said. 'I was thinking, how about no allowance for the rest of the year?'

'Dishes every night, including pots and pans. Even when you burn stuff,' said Lana to her dad.

'No more snicker doodles for me. Ever,' Buzz said gravely to my mother.

'My goodness,' she said. 'That's quite a sacrifice, Buzzy.'

'We know we were totally out of line,' I said, 'and we're ready to accept whatever you think we deserve.'

'And after you decide our fate, we want you to just disregard what you witnessed last night, and strike it from the record,' Buzz said.

I groaned internally. Sometimes Buzz has a way of taking things too far.

'Disregard what?' my mother said.

'You know, the whole incompatability thing,' Buzz explained.

'What Buzz is trying to say, even though he shouldn't really be saying anything *at all*,' I said, giving him a pointed look, 'is that we hope you can just forget about last night.'

'Oh, no, that would be impossible. What

happened last night has changed everything. We're not ever going to be able to forget about it,' my mother said.

Was I hearing this right? Were the pieces falling into place just the way I'd thought they would? Yahoo! Score one for the three blabbing lawyers.

'That's right,' said Jerry. 'What we learned last night has made us realise that we are even more right for each other than we'd dared to hope.'

I heard screeching brakes in my head.

'*What?*' I managed to say.

'He's right. Your wonderful, disastrous little dinner party last night made us even more certain that this marriage is the right thing for all of us. Didn't it, honeybunch?' she said, leaning over and putting her cheek against the top of Jerry's head.

'Mmm-hmm,' he said, reaching up and touching her face.

How could this be happening?

'You mean even after everything you saw last night, you're still planning to . . . to . . .' Lana stammered.

'Marry? Absolutely!' my mother said, throwing her arms around Jerry and giving him a big kiss on the cheek. 'Turns out that both of us have been a little worried that maybe we were a bit *too* compatible. We know from experience that a good marriage has to be strong enough to survive a little conflict now and then. We'd never had a fight before last night, not even a spat. And now that we have, we know we can kiss and make up even after a whopper. We're both so relieved. And grateful.'

This was getting worse by the minute. Not only were they still getting married, but they were also *grateful* to us for bringing them even closer together.

'And you know what the frosting on the cake is?' Jerry went on.

I wasn't sure I could bear hearing it.

'Seeing you and Lana working together so beautifully last night. It made us realise that you two have kissed and made up too.'

Lana began to wheeze at the other end of the couch.

'We're now totally convinced,' my mother said happily, 'that we are all ready to be—'

Lana and I both knew what she was about to say and instinctively covered our ears. Only Buzz heard my mother and Jerry finish the sentence in blissful unison:

'One big happy family!'

CHAPTER FIFTEEN

What happened next was pretty surprising. Lana stopped wheezing just long enough to haul off and punch me right in the eye.

'Here's some real frosting for your cake, Daddy,' she yelled as she ran out of the room, out the door, and outside without even putting her jacket on. Jerry and Buzz took off after her, leaving me alone with my mother.

'Oh, honeybunch,' she said, rushing over to look at my eye. 'Are you okay?'

It hurt like crazy, and I wasn't at all sure that I was going to be okay. My mother ran out into the kitchen and came back with a square chunk of something white and slimy in her hands.

'Here, Guysie, put this on your eye.'

'What is that?' I said, rolling around on the couch in pain, holding my face and moaning.

'It's tofu,' she said. 'You're supposed to put a raw steak on a black eye, but this is all I have. It's organic. Just put it on and hold it there,' she said. 'You poor, poor baby.'

I did what she told me to do, but it didn't help at all and it smelled disgusting.

'One thing is clear: that girl is going to need to do some serious work on her temper,' my mother said, taking the tofu out of my hand and putting it down on the coffee table in front of the couch. She leaned over me, slipped on her reading glasses – the pink sparkly ones that always hang around her neck on a shoestring – and examined my rapidly swelling eye. 'She probably has too much food colouring in her diet.'

'Mom, why do you say stuff like that?' I asked, pushing her hands away from my face.

'It's a well-documented fact that diet can have a very profound effect on human moods,' she said. 'I read an article just last week about those little fruit snacks kids take in their lunch boxes being linked to depression. Especially the blue ones. It was a very convincing piece of—'

'Mom!' I shouted. 'Why are you talking about fruit snacks? You're ruining my life and all you can think about is food colouring. Your future daughter, the one you think it would be so nice to have around the house, just punched me in the face. Don't you even care?'

'Of course I care,' my mother said. 'And believe me, I'm going to see to it that it never happens again. I'm sure Jerry is out there talking to Lana right now about controlling her temper in the future.'

'The *future*?' I said. 'What future? Mine is totally doomed because of what you're doing. How can you sit there pretending that you care when you're going ahead and marrying Jerry even though I've told you that I don't want you to?'

'I know you're having trouble accepting my decision, Guy. But you have to believe me when I say that I want you to be happy. I want all of us to be happy. And I really think that with time you'll adjust to this change and you'll see that we can all be—'

'If you say "one big happy family" one more time, I'm going to scream so loud the roof is gonna fly right off this house!' I shouted at the top of my lungs.

My mother was quiet. The front door opened and my dad came in with Sweetie Pie Dough. Sweetie lifted his nose in the air and started sniffing, quickly locating the tofu on the table and managing to snatch it and gobble it down before my mother could stop him. Afterwards he stood there licking his chops and wagging his tail at her.

'What's going on in here?' my father asked, unzipping his jacket and coming into the room. 'I could hear Guy yelling halfway down the block' Then he caught sight of my eye. 'Holy cow, what happened to you?'

'Lana punched me,' I said.

'Are you all right, Guychick?' he asked, coming over and sitting down on the couch next to me.

'No, Dad. I'm not. But nobody really cares.' I started to cry but I had to stop myself right away because it hurt my bad eye too much when I wrinkled up my face and I couldn't seem to cry without doing it.

The front door opened again and Lana, Jerry, and Buzz came in.

'How is Guy?' Jerry asked from the hall.

'He's okay, honeybunch,' she answered. 'But he's probably going to have a black eye.'

'Lana, you have something to say to Guy, don't you?' Jerry said sternly.

Lana cleared her throat. She was still wheezing a little, and I could tell she'd been crying.

'Don't bother. I'm not interested in anything any of you have to say,' I said as I stood up with my hand over my throbbing eye. 'Instead you can all listen to what I have to say for a change. I'm not doing it. I'm not living in this house with you people. Mom, you go ahead and marry Jerry if you want, but you can forget about having me around any more. I quit. I'm not putting up with this. I'm outta here.'

'I think maybe my Guy and I need some private time together,' my mother said softly.

'Forget it. I don't want to spend any private time with you, Mom. Or any other kind of time either. And quit calling me *your* Guy. I'm not yours. Not any more. I hope you have a good life with *your* Jerry and *your* Lana, but you can leave me out of it from now on.'

And with that I pushed past my mother and all the rest of them and ran up to my room, slamming the door behind me.

Buzz knocked a minute later.

'Hey, Guy Wire,' he called softly. 'Can I come in?'

'No, go away,' I called back.

'Come on. Can't I at least come in and watch your eye turn colours?' he said.

'Go away,' I said, and I guess he could tell I meant it, because a few seconds later I heard him move away from the door and go back downstairs.

A minute or so after that my mother tapped on the door and came in, even though I hadn't told her it was okay to.

'Guysie, we need to talk,' she said.

'About what? There's nothing to say. You've made your decision. Now go away and leave me alone.'

'Look, I handled this the wrong way – I can see that now. I should have told you about Jerry and me right away so you could have had time to get used to him before we popped the news about our engagement. I'm sorry I didn't think it through clearly. But you know how I am sometimes.'

'*Sometimes?*' I said. 'Mom, you're always like this. You never think things through. You just do whatever you feel like doing and expect me to deal with it.'

My mother was quiet for a minute. She kept biting her lower lip until there was no lipstick left on it.

'I'm sorry you're hurt,' she said softly.

'Sorry enough not to go through with it?' I asked.

'You mean not to get married? No. You have to understand – I love him, Guy.'

'And you have to understand – I *hate* him,' I said. 'And his horrible daughter, too.'

'But you and Lana seemed to be getting along so well last night,' she said.

'That was an act, Mom. Look at my eye. Don't you get it? We were only working together so that we wouldn't have to *be* together. A lot of good it did us. After all we went through, you're still going to marry that, that *clown*.'

'Is that what bothers you about him, Guy? That he's a clown?'

'Everything about him bothers me. His horrible jokes. That stupid plastic fly. The way he looks. The fact that he's Lana father. And the way, the way you . . .'

I suddenly started to choke up, which made me wince with pain.

'The way I what, Guysie?' my mother asked gently.

I wasn't sure I could get it out.

'Tell me,' she said. 'Please.'

'The way you call him "*honeybunch*".' Hot tears spilled down my cheeks. 'That's what you call *me* – don't you even know that?'

'Oh, Guysie. I'm sorry.' She sat down on the edge of the bed and tried to hug me. 'I didn't even realise.'

'So what else is new?' I said sarcastically as I rolled away from her to the other side of the bed, where I faced the wall.

'I want you to be happy, Guy.'

'Well, I'm not. And the one thing that could make me happy you're not willing to do,' I said.

'You mean not get married?' she said.

'Yes, at least not now. And not to him.'

'Do you really think you'd be okay with anyone else I might want to marry?' she asked me. 'Seems to me you haven't liked any of the men I've dated since your dad and I split up.'

'What do you expect, Mom? They're all weirdos. The only guy you've ever liked that I like too is Dad. And you kicked him out.'

'I didn't exactly kick him out,' my mother said. 'We drifted apart and found that we no longer—'

'Oh, blah, blah, blah,' I said. 'However you

want to put it, he's not here any more and you had something to do with it.'

She was quiet.

'Knock, knock,' my father said softly as he stuck his head in the door. Sweetie was with him, and he came in and jumped up in my mother's lap. 'How's the eye, Guychick?'

'My eye is the least of my problems,' I said. 'The question is how's my life? And the answer is *over.* Mom is going to marry her clown, I'll have to live here being tortured by his bad jokes and in constant fear that Lana is going to punch my lights out, and there's nothing anybody can do about it. My life is ruined. Totally ruined. *Unless* . . .' I sat up. Why hadn't I thought of this before? 'Unless you let me move in with you, Dad.'

'Now, Guy, you know your father has to travel all the time. That's why we've set it up the way we have, with you being here with me. You can't be alone when he—'

'Hang on a second, Lorraine,' my father said slowly. 'Maybe he's onto something here.

I've actually been wanting to cut back on my travelling. There's really no reason Guy couldn't come live with me the way he's been living with you this past year.'

'What do you mean?' my mother said anxiously.

'You've had Guy with you most of this past year, Lorraine. When you think about it, it's only fair for me to have a chance to be with him like that too.'

'You can't possibly think I'd let Guy move out.'

'Why not?' I said excitedly. 'That would solve everything, and I'd never even have to see those stupid Zuckermans.'

'Hold on a second, Guy,' said my dad. 'You'd still spend time with your mother, the same as you have been with me. Occasional weekends and school vacations.'

'Would I have to?' I asked. 'Couldn't I just stay with Buzz for those times?'

When I said that, my mother burst into tears and ran out of the room. Sweetie jumped down and quickly followed after her.

'That was a little harsh, Guychick,' my father said.

I didn't say anything.

'You know, your mother loves you very much. She wants you to be happy. She's just sort of between a rock and a hard place right now.'

'I don't care,' I said, folding my arms across my chest and leaning back against the wall.

'Yes you do,' he said, reaching out and pushing the damp hair off my forehead. 'Listen, why don't you get some rest now, and I'll be back to check on you in a while. Your mother and I need to talk.'

'About me moving in with you?' I asked.

'Well, yes. This is all kind of sudden, and it's pretty clear from her reaction that she's not wild about the idea.'

'But you are, right?'

'I think it'd be great for you and me to be able to spend more time together, Guychick. But your mom and I need to talk it through. Let me go do that now, okay? I'll check back with you when we're done.'

'Dad?' I said.

'Yes?' he said, pausing with his hand on the doorknob.

'Don't let her talk you out of it. Please. You're my only hope.'

CHAPTER SIXTEEN

So my parents talked it over, and surprisingly enough, my mother didn't manage to convince my father to change his mind. Well, at least not all the way. What they came up with was a compromise – a new arrangement where I would spend one week living with my mom and then the next week I'd be with my dad. It meant that I still had to deal with Lana and Jerry, but at least every other week I'd be getting a break from it.

'The only drawback as far as I can see is the food,' Buzz said one day after school, as we sat up on the loft bed in my room at my dad's, eating a bag of store-bought gingersnaps.

'What do you mean?' I said.

He leaned over the edge of the bed and pitched a half-eaten cookie into my waste-basket. 'These cookies stink. It's like eating spicy checkers. Can't your mom teach your dad how to bake cookies for the weeks that you're staying with him?'

'My dad only knows how to make one thing from scratch – scrambled eggs. And half the time he burns them, so don't be holding your breath for homemade cookies around here, Buzzard.'

'If he can't cook, then how come there are two big cans of chicken broth out on the coffee table in the living room? Looks to me like he's got something other than frozen dinners in mind for dinner tonight.'

'Wrong again, Buzzard. He uses those for barbells. This morning when I got up, he was out there exercising in his underwear, lifting the cans over his head and marching around to an Alvin and the Chipmunks tape he bought at a yard sale last weekend.'

Buzz shook his head.

'Remember when we thought he'd had a total personality change and wasn't weird any more?' he said.

'Some things never change,' I said.

The truth is I'm glad my dad is still a little wacky. He's a lot of fun to hang out with, and it's nice getting to see him more. Buzz is right about the food at his house, but we both like pizza and Chinese takeout, so we do all right.

'Has your mom finished Lana's room yet?' Buzz asked.

'Yep,' I said. 'We have to eat all our meals in the kitchen now, or sometimes out in the living room with plates on our laps. When they actually move in, it's going to be really tight.'

My mother had covered the glass doors in the dining room with lacy curtains, and she and Jerry had painted the room pink over the weekend. It was way too frilly for my taste, but I was just glad nobody had suggested Lana take over my room since I was only going to be there half as much time as she was.

'Have you decided about the wedding?' Buzz asked me. 'Are you going?'

'I haven't made up my mind yet,' I said. 'My mom wanted me to carry the rings for the ceremony on a little pillow, but I said no. She says she hopes I'll at least come, but I'm not sure.'

'It's soon,' Buzz said.

'Yeah. Next week. Valentine's Day.'

'I got an invitation,' he said.

'Really? Are you gonna go?'

'If you want me to,' he said.

'Well, maybe I'll go if I can sit in the back with you.'

'Uh, I kind of promised Lana I'd sit with her,' Buzz said.

'Oh, great,' I said. 'Then forget it.'

'You know, she's really sorry about your eye.'

'I know, I know. She wrote me a pretty nice letter apologising. But who knows, maybe she only did it 'cause her dad made her.'

'No, I'm sure she wrote you the letter because she's genuinely sorry she punched you. And she even promised never to call you Girlie Guy for the rest of your life, right?'

'How do you know that?' I asked, looking at him suspiciously. 'I never showed you the letter.'

Buzz blushed.

'I sort of helped her write it,' he said.

'I should have known.'

'You know, she's not as bad as you think she is. She told me you even admitted that yourself right before she punched you.'

'What are you talking about?' I asked.

'She said you told her you didn't want to be her brother, but she wasn't quite as bad as you thought she was.'

'Whatever,' I said.

Just then there was a scratching sound at the door. I climbed down the ladder and opened the door. Sweetie Pie Dough came clicking in, wagging his little plume of a tail. Sweetie, as it turned out, had officially become my dad's dog. When the dust had settled and I finally got around to admitting to my mother that I hadn't really called the pound to report that we'd found

Sweetie, she called them right up, apologised for the delay, and gave them a complete description, including the part about his being exceptionally bright. But no one ever came to claim him. At first my mom wanted to keep him. She was sure she could teach him to like Jerry. But no amount of coaxing or peanut butter cracker rewards could convince Sweetie to stop biting Jerry every time he got the chance, so my mom finally asked my dad if he would be willing to adopt the dog. That way, she said, we could at least keep him in the family.

'So are things getting any better between you and Jerry?' Buzz asked.

'My mom made him promise not to do fly tricks when I'm around, and that helps a little. But I'm still not wild about him.'

'Isn't there *anything* good about him?' Buzz asked.

'You mean, like, can he move pianos?' I said.

Buzz laughed.

'Actually, there is one thing,' I said. 'He can make music out of junk.'

'What are you talking about?'

'Because of his piccolo playing, I guess, he's got this special way of putting his lips on things and blowing into them that makes music come out,' I explained.

'What kind of things does he blow into?' asked Buzz.

'Junk. Like hoses and bolts and funnels. Last night he played Beethoven on my mother's plant mister, and it sounded pretty good.'

'That's cool.'

'Yeah, it is, but he's still a dork,' I said.

'Okay. But a dork with talent is better than a dork without talent, right?'

'I guess. Besides which, he and my mom do seem really happy. It's kind of sickening, but I only have to be around it every other week.'

'Hey, Sweetie,' Buzz called down from the loft. 'Play dead for your Uncle Buzzy.'

Sweetie did it willingly.

'Garbanzo!' Buzz cried delightedly, tossing him a gingersnap. 'Keep it up and you may hit the big time, just like Max Soggy Underpants. Speaking of which, Guy Wire, did you hear that Autumn gave him the slip? Lana told me Autumn thinks he's conceited now.'

I have to admit I was kind of happy to hear that.

'Hey, guess what else?' Buzz said as he swung his legs over the side of the loft and jumped down next to me with a loud thud. 'Somebody finally bought the Petersons' house – you know, the nice one next door to me with the swimming pool in the backyard. I saw them putting up the SOLD sign out front this morning.'

'Huh. Maybe they'll have a halfway decent kid our age. And maybe he'll let us swim in his pool this summer,' I said.

'Yeah,' said Buzz. 'That would be cool. When the Petersons lived there, they never let any kids swim in the pool 'cause they didn't think we could be trusted not to pee in it.'

'In your case it might have been true,' I said.

'Very funny. Hey, I gotta go. My mom told me if I don't clean up my room today, she's going to send me to a farm to live with my own kind.'

'Relatives, you mean?' I asked.

'No, you Grapenut – pigs.'

'Okay, Porky, go sweep up,' I said.

I walked Buzz to the door. When he was halfway down the porch steps, he turned around.

'Think about coming to the wedding, will ya?' he said. 'I'll tell Lana I'm gonna sit with you. She'll understand. Besides, the fact is that your mom will be really disappointed if you don't come, and you know since she's planned the whole thing, chances are pretty good it's gonna be a real humdinger.'

He was certainly right about that.

CHAPTER SEVENTEEN

'What the heck is this music?' Buzz whispered to me. 'Don't they usually play the organ at things like this?'

We were sitting next to each other in the back of the tiny little neighbourhood church Jerry and my mother had decided to get married in. They'd only invited a few neighbours and friends, so it wasn't a big crowd. Mr and Mrs Adams, Buzz's parents, were sitting up near the front. I was wearing my good suit, which I had refused to try on beforehand and was now paying the price for because apparently I'd grown about five inches since the last time I'd worn it. The trousers were way too short, and it was so tight I could barely move. I'd already torn the jacket riding over to the church from my dad's house on the handlebars of Buzz's bike.

'This music is one of my mother's favourite tapes. Tribal drumming,' I explained. 'She says it awakens the beast in her.'

'I'll bet,' Buzz said as he rolled his eyes.

'Speaking of wild animals, where's Lana, anyway?' I asked.

'Very funny. I'm not sure. She said she'd be here, but I don't see her.'

'Was she mad about you sitting with me?' I asked.

'No. She said she had some job she had to do anyway.'

Suddenly the drumming stopped and the whole room was filled with an unearthly, high-pitched sound. It was actually beautiful in a way, and it seemed to whistle over our heads, bouncing off the walls, colliding and folding back over itself again and again like musical waves. I'd never heard anything like it.

'Look!' whispered Buzz. 'It's Jerry.'

Sure enough, Jerry had come out wearing a tuxedo and a small polka-dot bow tie. I recognised the material right away. It was the same as his clown suit. He was cupping his hands around an object into which he was blowing and making that music. When he finished and pulled the instrument away from his lips, I saw that it was a hose nozzle.

Lana appeared at the head of the aisle with a large wicker basket in her arms. She was wearing a long pink dress I was willing to bet my mother had made for her, since it had little bride and groom dolls glued all the way around the bottom of it. They clicked and clattered together noisily as she walked down the aisle, reaching into the basket periodically to pull out big white rose petals, which she sprinkled on the red carpet running the length of the church.

She seemed kind of nervous, and she didn't even look at us as she walked by. Buzz reached down after she'd passed and picked up one of the rose petals.

'Hey, what's this?' he said, handing it to me.

But before I could answer him, Jerry started playing on the nozzle again and my mother appeared in the doorway, ready to walk down the aisle toward him.

'Sheesh-a-rama!' exclaimed Buzz, poking me hard in the ribs. 'What the heck is she wearing?'

As you might expect, my mother had designed her own dress. And like Jerry's hose-nozzle music, it was unique, to put it mildly.

'Is it my imagination, or are those Styrofoam cups she's got all over her?' Buzz asked.

'I'm not positive, but I'm pretty sure those "rose petals" Lana's throwing around are pieces of Styrofoam plates, so I'm beginning to sense a theme here,' I said.

I watched my mother as she began to walk down the aisle. I wouldn't have thought it possible for someone to look beautiful wearing a bunch of Styrofoam cups, but she did. Her red hair was piled up in a fancy way on top of her head, and when she caught sight of me, I saw her eyes fill with tears and she broke into a huge smile. She kept walking, but when she got to our row, she paused.

'*Cool dress!*' Buzz whispered, giving her a thumbs-up sign.

She smiled at him. Then she leaned down, her Styrofoam cups squeaking a little as they rubbed against each other, and she whispered in my ear, 'I don't care what you say. No matter what, you will always be my Guy.'

Then she hugged me, and I hugged her back right there in front of everybody. After a minute she stood up, straightened her dress, and continued down the aisle to Jerry, who was waiting with the judge at the front of the church.

I had been right. There was a theme, and it culminated in a poem that my mother had written for Jerry and recited right before they exchanged rings.

> '*Most things on earth come and go,*
> *Ebb and flow like the sea,*
> *But our love is like Styrofoam,*
> *Here for all eternity.*'

It was a short ceremony, and afterward we were all supposed to meet at a nearby restaurant for cake and dancing. I certainly didn't intend to dance, and I knew I couldn't take a chance on eating anything because my trousers were already dangerously tight.

My mother and Jerry walked out of the church in a shower of not rice, but Styrofoam packing peanuts as guests tossed handfuls of them, which they scooped out of big bowls that had been set out on the steps for that purpose.

Jerry's station wagon had Styrofoam coffee cups on strings tied to the rear bumper instead of tin cans, and the sign in the back window said JUST MARRIED (AGAIN).

Buzz and I stood at the top of the steps, taking in the scene. Lana came over and joined us.

'Have you forgiven me for punching you yet?' she said to me.

'Yeah,' I said. 'Pretty much.'

'Good. Your eye doesn't look bad today. Can't say the same for that suit, though.'

I laughed.

'You should talk. That's quite a dress you've got on there.'

'Isn't it?' She held out her skirt and twirled around once, making an awful racket as the plastic dolls knocked together. 'Your mother made it for me – can you tell? She's completely insane.'

'Tell me about it,' I said.

'She was planning to glue on a bunch of other stuff too, but I hid her glue gun under the couch the last time I was over there so she wouldn't be able to.'

I laughed.

Buzz looked overjoyed that we were getting along so well.

'You did a great job throwing around those petals, Your High-ness,' Buzz said. 'And even though the dress is a little weird, you look pretty.'

'Thanks,' said Lana.

'Guysie!' my mother called up to me from the kerb, where she and Jerry were getting ready to get into the car. 'Why don't you and Lana come ride with us?'

'Are you coming to the restaurant?' I asked Buzz.

'Yeah. But I think I'm going to go home for a minute first and change my clothes. This get-up is too uncomfortable,' he said, tugging at the tie around his neck.

'Lana! Guy! Hurry up!' my mother called.

'See you over there, Buzzer,' Lana said.

Then she took him completely by surprise by giving him a quick peck on the cheek. He turned a deep shade of pink I'd never seen him achieve before.

'Sheesh,' he said softly.

Lana and I ran down the steps and got in the back seat.

'Mom, can we stop at the house so I can change out of my suit real quick before the party? Buzz is doing it too,' I said.

'Yeah, no offence, Lorraine, but this dress is too noisy to walk around in all night. Can we stop at our house too, Daddy, so I can change?'

'Okay, we'll do that,' my mother said.

Jerry turned the car around and started up

the street. But he wasn't heading toward my mother's house or in the direction of his own house either.

'How come we're going this way?' I asked.

My mother turned around in her seat and smiled at me.

'Where are we going, Dad?' Lana said.

'You'll see,' Jerry sang.

I looked at Lana and she shrugged. A minute later Jerry pulled over, stopped, and turned off the engine.

'Here we are,' my mother said.

'Here we are where?' I asked.

'This is it,' said Jerry.

'What?' asked Lana. 'This is what?'

'This is our new house,' my mother said, turning around to see Lana's and my reactions.

'You've got to be kidding!' I shouted.

'Nope,' said my mother, holding up three fingers. 'Girl Scout's honour. After I finished converting the dining room into a bedroom for Lana, we realised the house is just too small for four people. Even though I know you're only going to be spending half your time there, Guysie, I want the time that you are with me, with us, to be as nice as it can be. So – this is it. Our new house.'

'You guys aren't joking, are you, Dad? Because if you are, that would really not be funny,' Lana said.

'We signed the papers last week, honey. Girl Scout's honour,' he said, holding up the wrong three fingers.

My mother reached over and corrected him, gently folding his pinkie and thumb down and then leaving her hand on his. They smiled at each other.

'So, what do you think?' my mother said, turning around again toward us.

'Awesome,' Lana and I said together.

'Don't you two want to get out and go check out the place?' asked Jerry.

'Absolutely, but first, can I borrow your cell phone for a minute?' I asked him.

Jerry unclipped the phone from his belt and handed it over the back of the seat to me. Then he reached over and patted my mom's cheek. She was beaming.

'Come on, Lana,' I said, opening the car door. 'We've got an important call to make.'

'Let me do it,' she said, reaching for the phone.

'Well, I kind of wanted to be the one – oh, okay.' I handed her the phone.

She held it for a second and then handed it back to me.

'No, that's okay, Guy. You can make the call.'

'Thanks.'

We ran across the yard together around the side of the house and into the backyard. I punched in the numbers and waited while it rang.

'Hello! Yo, Buzz Cut, it's me. You know those new neighbours of yours, the ones who just moved into that great big house next door to you? Well, two of them are outside standing in the middle of their empty swimming pool . . . Never mind how I know. Hang up and go look out the window!'

Lana and I had climbed down the ladder and were standing in the deep end of the empty pool. We waved furiously when we caught sight of Buzz hanging his head out the window. Even from that far away I could see his jaw drop open in shock, and then a big smile spread across his face.

'Can you believe it?' I yelled over to him. 'We're gonna be neighbours!'

He pumped his fist in the air and yelled something back at me that made me laugh.

'What did he say, Guy?' Lana asked. 'Was it something about bongos?'

'No,' I said with a big grin. 'He said *garbanzo*.'

And I couldn't have put it better myself.